Dedicated to my mom and dad, and all those who choose to see everyone as one of "us", and not to be afraid of "them."

Preface

A Poem

I saw him again.

Today.

He was about my same height.

His complexion was darker than those around him and he stood out from the surrounding crowd of shoppers.

His clothes had a shabbiness that also stood out – a bland tannish brown coat and matching dull pants made of some loose, coarse material like burlap bags sewn together. Scratchy-looking like recycled towels. They were clothes purchased from a generic clothing store of generic design of generic materials for generic people.

I sensed the smell – the distinctive bouquet of unwashed human – a scent that must have repulsed predators, long ago … an ancient smell from when we lived in caves … like animals … when each person's smell joined forces with the smell of others comprising a battalion of reek.

A protective wall of stench.

Strong human stench.

Primal.

Feral.

Disgusting.

Old sweat, bacteria, filth, residue of feces, tones of urine, all interwoven with a fragrance of indifference … or maybe an aroma of acceptance. I sensed this is how

MIRROR MIRROR

A MYSTERY

BERNIE NOFEL

Art direction, design, and
production managment by:

he smelled – knew it was how he smelled exactly – but managed from habit to turn off my nose.

As best I could.

His face was mottled, like a craggy seashore cliff. Buffeted into form and shape by seconds, hours, and years – each hourglass grain leaving behind a permanent reminder of wear, and want, and insult. His skin was calloused, hardened — a tough shell encasing fragile innards like an insect's exoskeleton. It grew to protect him from on-shore winds and winter storms but yielded to inevitable cracks where joints, requiring movement, are designed for a more supple encasement. And so leave creased cracks in their wake as they bend, over and over.

The waves of time-passed-torturously folded over and again into permanent crevices on that face.

His eyes were calloused too. They had squinted under summer's relentless sun and grown accustomed to looking at masses of people who never looked back – eyes that looked outward and were never looked into – eyes that had long-since seen there was no hope that they, themselves would ever really be seen by others.

"I am invisible, you know." A voice. Had I been staring?

His face cracked into a half-grin, more out of conditioning than mirth, and the worn cracks around his mouth revealed a few teeth, the few he had, which are not worth describing.

"Heh, heh, heh," a sandpaper voice shaped by cigarettes, booze, and hard times let out what was intended to be a chuckle.

I reached into my pocket to initiate a transaction of escape, to pay off my conscience and buy permission to return to the place where the washed, and the busy, and the proper, and the smiling walked by in the world that is the world and not the non-world of the invisible. Of the feral.

To purchase through miniscule, self-indulgent "charity" a ticket away from this walking dark plot twist and so, then… on my way.

Away.

Away.

He grabbed my wrist.

I was frozen. I was fixed. I was a mannikin. His hand was course and barnacled – it felt more like a horse's hoof than skin, and his grip wasn't particularly strong but it imprisoned me nonetheless – and passersby passed by, and pedestrians perambulated, and strollers breezed along and none took note of this unfolding capture. None took note of my abduction into this other place, none felt the choking clump growing in my throat, no one saw the chilly beads of sweat that blossomed on my face, could see the obvious – that inside my mouth had grown a field of cotton, that I was a man drowning in the ocean hoping for a lifeguard….

"May I tell you something?" the voice again.

I believe I nodded.

"Don't you think it's strange that we keep seeing each other?"

And I'm outside a store in the Fashion Valley Mall. I vaguely sense what type of store I am staring at – I believe it's a boutique shaving company. I smell an ancient protectant smell. I see the people of the normal world.

The storefront has a nice reflection. I see a man holding his wrist. I see myself holding my wrist. I see one person in the mirror. No one else. Just me. Holding my own wrist.

And the people passing by hear me talking to myself.

1

The Other is the Other.

That is all.

"The Other is the Other," said the Other. "That is all."

The Other is not Us. Not one of us.

"Less than," whispered the Other. "We are not the Other. Or so we believe. Or so we need to believe."

The Other is the Other.

That is all.

2

Vanessa Altuve loved to sweat. Craved it. Yearned for it. Needed to "work up a lather".

Push, push, – propel herself over space. Loved the feel of being hot – working, pumping, breathing heavy, challenging herself. More than getting her physical fix.

Vanessa needed to rise above.

Today was Monday so it was an early morning run. Like anyone else, she never felt like getting up. No one's body wants to leave the comfort of a warm and secure bed at 5 AM, particularly to exchange their blanketed warm cocoon for the early chill of an October morning in Cleveland.

"Mind leads, body follows" Tiffany yawned out to her phone, whose gentle wakeup call this morning was "*Sober*" by Tool. A rooster on her windowsill would be less jarring.

"Mind leads, body follows." She gritted her whole body and didn't rise out of bed – she *sprang* out of it, like an angry cat.

Vanessa walked to the bathroom, peed, washed her hands, brushed her teeth, took off her shirt, and splashed cold water on her face and over her naked chest and shoulders.

She shuddered, gritted again, dried off, put on her running bra, her running shorts and shoes, her headphones, and said it again, only this time she said it the way she learned it from her father. The way she had it tattooed on her arms. *"Mente lleva"* on her left arm. *"Cuerpo sigue"* on her right.

When she said it that way, she kissed the cross on her necklace and thought of … her father. She thought of him like this every single time. How as a young girl, her father would already be awake when it was still dark. She remembered him as so caring. Her protective guardian. Her rock. Her *amorosa roca*.

In the morning, her rock, getting ready to work the first of the two jobs he always had.

She remembered him today. Clean from a shower. Smelling different when he came home. Always smelling like dad.

"Daddy, why are you up so early?" she would ask with half-open eyes. "You come home so late. Don't daddies need to sleep too?"

"My little one. Your father will do for you, my precious. What needs to be done, I will always do. You are my heart, and without a heart a man cannot live. Now, you get ready for school so you can grow up and not have to work so hard like your poor father." And his eyes were so warm and tender that little Vanessa would feel like she was still under the blankets. And her father made her feel like that all day long, like she was tucked in and secure and safe.

Always.

Would feel that way as her father worked at the garage and come home smelling of grease and oil. Would feel that way when he would work all day filling baskets with strawberries, coming home smelling like fruit and sweat with an overtone of something sweet, like something people shouldn't be smelling like. Something used to kill bugs.

Químicos.

She would feel that way when she, herself, studied long into the night waiting for her father to come home. Would feel that way when he would walk in the door, and his short, strong body would drag in a tired face until he saw his little "Nessa'" and the exhaustion would leave his face and she knew. She knew. That her face made him feel like he was already under the blankets himself, and secure, and home.

Home.

And loved.

For a while. A short while. Until he had to drive himself through another day. Another morning.

When he would tell his sleepy little one the same thing again, "*mente lleva, cuerpo sigue.*"

"*Mi amado padre*" Vanessa whispered into the dark. In her running gear now. Her words forming little vapor clouds in the crisp Cleveland air. Outside in a sharp October morning. The sun still an hour or so from peeking out. She made the sign of cross. "Mind leads, body follows, right papa?"

And, off she ran.

"You're living in your own Private Idaho, your own Private Idaho!" The B52's in her headphones, she pushed the pace right from the start. Thoughts of her late father were near and warming this morning. How grateful she was that he got to see her graduate. How impossible it still seems that her rock finally eroded, chipped away by a life that had to constantly endure storms and wind and rain, like a cliff along the beach.

"Pesticide-related illness," it said on the death certificate. "Final settlement," it later said on the check from the company. And, they cashed the few dollars on that check.

"This is what they say your papa's life is worth," she remembers her Tia saying.

This is what her papa's life is worth.

Vanessa looked at her watch. First mile at 6:52. "Whoa girl, still got four more to go," and she backed off the pace just a little.

"Someday, Tia, I will make this stop. Someday, I will make sure that no one's papa has to go to heaven because of their job," and she wiped one tear – her last tear – and gritted her body for the future.

"I know, *mi querida sobrina*. I know" and her Tía pulled Vanessa into her ample bosom and Vanessa felt warm again, like she was under the covers, but this time the warmth was different. This was the beginning, the sparking, of a fire she only partly understood….

Today's case was against Monsanto. She grinned thinking about it. Vanessa's famous grin. There was nothing friendly about it. It was more the grin of a predator before it strikes. Or a snake before eating eggs from a nest. Cold. Ruthless. Unrelenting.

 It was the face she'd made studying late nights in the library for finals. It was the face she'd made before her entrance interview for law school. It was the grin she'd made before taking the Bar exam. It was the same face she made before sparring at her Muay Tai club.

Like a shark before gashing its teeth into unsuspecting prey. Hence, her nickname "*La tiburón*" and the shark tattoo on her right bicep. Vanessa was a shark. And, for her, there was always blood in the water.

And someone was gonna' pay.

She ran today through the Metroparks in the Cleveland suburb of North Royalton. She liked the way the squirrels looked up from their busy chatter like they recognized her. She liked seeing all the deer that were so plentiful in the area that homeowners considered them giant pests, little more than overgrown racoons. Her four-legged early morning companions knew well enough to leave her be. Deer are no match for a shark, even on land.

Most of all, she liked pushing herself when she knew others were sleeping.

Alone.

Hunting.

Getting an edge.

A shark's edge.

Relationships were for later, though she was a shark with men, as well. The hunter, not the prey, and she had enjoyed her share. But, they were all little more than candy – "appetite suppressants" she'd call them. She had bigger prey to catch. Always, a bigger corporate target to hunt. To make them stop hurting people.

Hers was a shark's path – solitary hunter. That was how she liked it. That was how she always ran.

Alone.

"Seven fifteen" Vanessa looked at her watch and grinned. Shark. She was back on pace. *Sabotage* from Beastie Boys came on her headphones. She loved her solitary sweat.

Only this run was going to be different. This run wasn't going to remain solitary. No, this run would include some unwelcome company. Very unwelcome company, indeed.

Vanessa Altuve, *la Tiburon*, was about to cross paths with the Other.

3

"Nigger come down this street, he gonna' die." Dave Acciarri laughed until snot came out of his nose. He always thought that was funny – funny in the way a cat thinks it's funny to take its time with a mouse. He rode his bicycle in frenetic mindless circles in front of Friendly Corners Beverages, located right in the heart of Cleveland's friendly Little Italy, 2020 Murray Hill Road.

Friendly, that is, if you happen to be the right color. Dave was the right color.

"Niggers stay in nigger town!" Joe La Grecca spat and threw a rock at Dave, which barely missed. Joe used to play baseball for Benedictine High School until he got "unenrolled." The priests at Benedictine never "expelled" any student. They certainly never "kicked anyone out." No, problem students whose behaviors couldn't be shaped by the paddle were just unenrolled, like being erased. One day they are on the rolls. The next day…gone. Somewhere else. Just not with us any longer, like a character from a dream.

Wake up.

Poof.

Gone like never there.

Of course, Joe deserved it. He always hated the school right from the day when he first looked at the street sign. "Martin Luther King Ave?!? What the fuck?"

"Coonstreet High" he called it, although it was his dad's poetic talents that first coined the phrase. His upstanding father taught him all he knew about people. Good people. Bad people. White People. Black people. The first lesson. The last lesson.

"I even hate saying the word 'nigger'," Joe threw another rock and came closer to Dave this time. It skipped off the ground in front of his bike. Dave didn't flinch.

The third teen on the street was Ray Cardibello. People would say "That Ray, he's a good-looking boy." Black curly hair, blue eyes, chin dimple, 6 foot, 190 chiseled pounds. Hair greased and combed. T shirt with rolled up sleeves and rolled up jeans. Leather jacket. He'd already gotten two girls in the neighborhood, as they said in those days, "in trouble". And it was handled the way it was handled in those days. The girls left for a while to visit family who lived out of town.

"For not liking to say nigger, you sure say nigger a lot," Ray lit up a Camel. Dave and Joe laughed at that one. They always laughed at Ray's jokes. Everyone did. Not that they were funny. Just something about Ray that made everyone want to be part of what was happening – to catch just a piece of the stardust that sprinkled off that good-looking boy – to catch pieces of luck that drifted off of him like dust motes hover off a couch on a sunny day.

They were the Ambassadors of Little Italy. Like Ambassadors, they were sure to greet anyone coming down Murray Hill Road. If you were white and okay, you got to the end of the street. If you were Black, you were greeted … differently. For those people, the Ambassadors rolled out the carpet. And the carpet was always red.

The Ambassadors were part of Jack Wharton's childhood. He sat on the curb in front of his parents' beverage store watching the three boys. He wasn't Italian, but because his parents delivered booze to the Ambassadors' homes ("family delivery"), Jack was safe. Not bulletproof safe. Just not-get-beat-up-so-long-he-was-invisible safe.

His family quietly went to synagogue, and gave generously to Holy Rosary Catholic Church, gave the biggest candy bars during Halloween, wrote a nice big check for the annual Parade of the Feast of the Assumption… and they otherwise stayed invisible too.

The year was 1983. Jack was 12 and this is where he learned who belonged. And who didn't. And where he was soon about to learn what he wanted to do. He had no way of knowing this sitting there invisible on the curb, but Jack was going to decide to become a cop.

4

The Other had been sitting in the Metroparks for several hours. "Patience is a virtue," he told himself and he believed in being virtuous. He hadn't moved. Still. Like a statue or mannikin. He sat with his knees to his chest wrapped in his arms for warmth.

The sky was cloudy, a gray static blanket hovering low

and silent and dark over Northern Ohio. A place where most people were still sleeping in bed. Under their blankets.

Warm.

Protected.

Safe.

He sat against a tree with the moss to his left so he faced Cleveland's East Side – the side of the Cuyahoga River where Cleveland's African-American families predominately lived. His clothes were covered in mud and he sat in mud. The park sounds had grown comfortable with him sitting there and all sorts of unknowable creatures chattered around in the bushes. Some were predators and some were prey. The Other liked thinking about that too.

Across the parkway, was a cacophony of disorganized trees and bushes. Hardscrabble bristles sticking up every which way like a man's face who'd been on vacation for a couple weeks and didn't care. They grew freely in any direction they wished, pushing and shoving their way forward, elbowing each other out of the way adamantly and with determination – their choice of where to grow may have been random but each branch was determined to go there anyway.

The Other scoffed at the plants' struggles to be free. "Freedom," he whispered barely audibly into the dark. "If freedom is something that has to be fought for, how can it really be free?" He thought silently to himself now and shifted his weight on his seat without noticeably moving. "Freedom is either free or it isn't real," he continued to debate in silence. "I know how to make freedom truly free. To make it a choice of staying together to survive. To accept each other as equals… or die."

Vanessa Altuve was in the zone. Beastie Boys always gave her an edgy feel as a runner, and she put a strut and pop in her stride through the North Royalton Metroparks. She was in her last mile now, and already rehearsing in her head her opening arguments. She had long since memorized every word, every citation of the law, every gesture, every moment of leaning over to give the judge just a glimpse of her cleavage before looking up quickly to catch his glance. She rehearsed it anyway. La Tiburon was always more prepared than she ever needed to be.

Cold blooded, calculating hunter.

The Other saw her coming. Could see her silhouette in the darkness. He knew someone would come along. Eventually. "Success comes easy to a patient man." His heart perked up, but only so much as he needed. His training came in handy in times like this. Composure under fire can be learned.

Vanessa's silhouette was barely visible in the darkness. The Other put on his night vision goggles, however, and she became a bright green. "Show time," he whispered. He poured half a pint of Southern Comfort on his pants, and staggered into the pathway where Vanessa was soon to approach.

Vanessa saw the figure up ahead, staggering around.

"Homeless," she thought and committed herself to adding a few more dollars to her monthly contribution at the local rescue mission. She wasn't afraid at all – she'd long since understood that most homeless people are more likely to be a victim of violence than a perpetrator. Weakened by deprivation, cowed by abuse – more likely to be scavenger/gatherers than hunters. And, if it came down to it, she was proficient in Muy Thai and regularly sparred with men.

Crossing the shark was a good way to come away bloody.

Nonetheless, Vanessa had a schedule to keep and had no intention of stopping or even slowing. Something strange about this dark figure, but also much that was familiar – the immediately recognizable uniform of the homeless – the costume of those not in the lower class or the lowest class, but those who are of the outcast.

Just as she was about to run by, however, the man who appeared so helpless took one quick stumble-step closer and piteously wailed two words. "Please help."

Vanessa Altuve had been raised in deprivation and poverty herself. Raised by a father who had taught her to see every human being as deserving of dignity. Raised her to always help others when she could. She couldn't just pass by another human being in need, no matter what the circumstances.

Not when they said … "please help."

Vanessa Altuve stopped.

5

Leroy Kelly Johnson could always run. Named after a Cleveland Browns running back great, he seemed to be able to run right out of the womb.

Born to run.

To run to daylight.

Leroy Kelly Johnson, aka "LK" or "44" by his friends, was a big 14-year-old. Like his namesake, he was a running back too, and had already shown unique athleticism as a 9th grader playing on the varsity. Had that rare spark on the field – that sense of invincibility – that always set the great ones apart.

He not only made it look easy, he took joy in making his opponent look silly. Less than. Beneath his regalness.

Not like him.

Mortal.

Jesters pursuing a mocking king.

A week earlier he had run "the gauntlet." Every freshman who started for Cleveland's Glenville High School football was challenged to face "the gauntlet" – the dare to run down Murray Hill Road from Ford Street to East 114th. For generations, "the gauntlet" was the ultimate dare, a challenge that only one out of ten, at most, had the courage or foolishness to attempt.

No, most freshman starters from Glenville High School

chose the ignominy of the alternative – wearing the pink cap during warmups for the Homecoming Football game. Better to wear the pink cap than to spill their red blood, is how most young men saw it.

It's not hard to understand why – 97.5% of the student population at Glenville High School identify as African-American. And everyone knew what would happen to any African American caught by the Ambassadors of Little Italy on Murray Hill Road.

Nonetheless, Leroy had successfully run the gauntlet.

Did it a week ago.

He was halfway down the road before anyone even spotted him. Joe La Grecca was the first. He had been sitting on a curb playing with a jar of wasps he'd caught in a jar when he saw the young Glenville running back streaking by.

Joe hollered "Hey coon! Hey coon! Hey coon!", ripped his pants getting off the curb, tripped, split his lip on the sidewalk, steadied himself with his hands, which scraped the pavement, and took off continuing to yell the Ambassador warning cry.

"Hey coon! Hey coon!"

Joe wasn't particularly fast and was even slower in his panic to catch the "coon". Leroy was quickly too far ahead to catch. Joe threw a rock which barely missed Leroy's head. Panting, he continued throwing rocks and yelling "Hey coon! Hey coon!" Leroy kept doing what Leroy did like Van Gogh just did what Van Gogh did.

Leroy ran.

Dave Acciarri heard the Ambassador call to duty and sprinted to the street with his special bat – the one with the spikes nailed into it. He got on his bicycle and took off after the sprinting "coon."

About three quarters of the way down Murray Hill Lane he saw the freshman from Glenville High and started gaining ground, laughing and screaming "Nigger! Nigger!" – he never got the hang of the Ambassador's official warning cry but loved screaming his favorite word.

Leroy had a nose for daylight, however, and got on the sidewalk. He zigzagged back and forth between fire hydrants, pedestrians, dogs without leashes that belonged to nobody, and garbage cans that were never brought inside. Running hard. In a full easy sprint. Smooth, balanced, gliding easily, faster and faster.

His stride was ... beautiful.

Dave followed on the sidewalk too – his heart was an Indy car and his legs pumped his Huffy like an enraged kangaroo. He'd closed on Leroy – 10 feet now, 6 – if he could just get beside the speedy Glenville boy, hit him just one time, bring him down like a lion bringing down a wildebeest – the others would come… and then the fun would begin.

Back and forth around and between the sidewalk obstacles Leroy sprinted – he wasn't scared as much as he was excited – he was a rabbit that had long since come to believe he would never be caught from behind by any fox.

Rabbits, though, don't usually try to run away from bicycles.

Dave swung his bat as he closed on Leroy and hit a light pole. "Goddamn it!" he swore and swung again, this time only catching air. Dave wasn't smart but he had a certain streetsmart – especially for causing pain.

He put his bat under his shoulder in a new strategy – he'd wait until he was right on top of this "coon" – close enough to where he couldn't miss. He pedaled and closed on the young running back from the other part of town.

Leroy was born to run, but Murray Hill Road from Ford Avenue to the safety of East 114th was longer than a football field. It was seven tenths of a mile – further than rabbits run – and his breathing got harder and his cuts between sidewalk obstacles became sluggish. The rabbit got tired, scared, and ran just as hard as when he started… just not as fast… and he knew it.

He then made a mistake.

He looked back.

And saw Dave's grin.

He saw Dave's bat.

He didn't see anyone willing to help.

He saw brick buildings pass by and wondered about the white folks who lived there. How many had been Ambassadors when they were teens? How many of their fathers?

Who started this?

He ran by a little girl in a white dress playing with a doll on the sidewalk. She looked up at him, saw his skin, lips, hair – all different, all worse – and ran off leaving her blond doll behind.

Dave raised his bat, now only a foot away. Reared it back, swung his nail-festooned weapon with a mixture of glee and rage, and "WOK!"

Dave found himself weightless, then bouncing, then pain and no pain, noise and no noise, and then there and not there.

Two hundred feet away, Joe LaGrecca couldn't believe his eyes. He'd been throwing rocks all during the chase, not thinking he'd actually hit anything, but he could throw and so he did… and hit his friend and fellow Ambassador in the back of his head in mid-swing.

He could see it all unfolding – the long arc of the rock soaring through the sky like an outfielder's heave to the plate. His friend on the bicycle swinging his bat forward. The blow to the head causing him to go limp. The momentum of the swing sending his fellow Ambassador forward, beyond the balance point, over the handlebars, his right leg up on the air, his left foot striking the sidewalk, his body jerking up, and then on the ground, tumbling over and over like a racecar that had taken a turn too fast – he looked like something Joe had seen in an Evil Knievel movie once – rolling over and over until finally coming to a stop in Mr. Luigi's rose bushes.

 "FUCK!" was all Joe La Grecca could say. "Fuck, fuck, fuck, fuck, FUCK!" and ran over to his friend who was just now regaining consciousness

The third Ambassador, Ray Cardibello, had been "making it" with the principal's daughter when the call to action came out. Ray was dedicated enough to stop, in mid-stroke if necessary, but still had to put on his pants (and give his hair a quick comb), which gave him just enough time to look out the window and see Dave tumbling around the street like a rodeo clown who had gotten too close to the bull.

"Fucking bozos," Ray swore, which made the principal's daughter laugh.

"You think this is funny?"

"No."

"Then, why are you laughing?"

"Cuz,…" and Ray grabbed the principal's daughter by the throat, pushed her head against the wall, and his eyes became viper's eyes … and he looked at her like she was a trapped mouse.

"Then don't laugh," he said in little more than a whisper. If someone only heard him say it – say if they overheard those words from the next room – they'd think it was just a suggestion.

Almost friendly.

But, there, in that room, coming from those frozen eyes, like staring into black ice on a dangerous road, the principal's daughter, unable to breath, understood.

This was no suggestion.

He left the terrified teen go, finished getting dressed, and walked outside to join his fellow, failed Ambassadors.

Leroy never knew what caused his pursuer on the bicycle to fall. He just figured Italians are too stupid to ride a bicycle. When he arrived with his friends on East 114th, there was the exuberant ritualistic celebratory ceremony – the crown, the hoisting, the victory dance (called the "WOP, WOP") – he would forever be known as someone who had survived the gauntlet.

That was last week.

But, Leroy wasn't satisfied. See, Leroy had run his whole life but this was one time he didn't feel good about running. Why should he have to run for his life on a public street? Why should he consider it normal to be chased just because he was Black? Why should he have to run from white people? Or anyone?

No, Leroy wasn't satisfied at all. And today, Leroy was going to get satisfaction. Today, he was going to do the gauntlet again. Only, this time the runner wasn't going to run. He was going to walk. Right down Murray Hill Road. Right down the middle of the street. With a couple of his boys. And a little something in his pocket in case someone came out to try to make him run.

"This time we walk," Leroy said to his three friends on Ford Avenue at the top of Murray Hill Road. "Heads up, shoulder to shoulder, like men." And the four 14-year-old "men" were committed.

Down Murray Hill Road they began to walk.

Right down the middle of the street.

Vanessa Altuve was born and raised in the bible by her father.

"*Como lo hiciste con uno de estos mis hermanos …*"

"As you did it to one of the least of these my brothers..." her papa would teach her…

"…*entonces tú me lo hiciste,*" she would reply.

"So you did it to me," she reminded herself as she interrupted her run to do as she'd been taught – been taught by her loving, hard-working papa – to see Christ in everyone, especially those who were the least of our brothers and sisters. And, this man in front of her now, reeking of booze and the rank mud he must have been sleeping it, was her brother now.

A brother in the Lord.

Vanessa Altuve had a busy day and a tight schedule. But, she could no more ignore this homeless man's plea for help any more than she could stop breathing – this wasn't just how she lived. It was her life. The way she learned to live from her papa. The way she would always live.

She would think of the people who could have helped him and turned away instead. She would never – NEVER – become one of them.

"I don't have any money with me when I run," she began and her voice, which could be so ruthlessly cutting in court, was as warm and nurturing as a new mother speaking to her child. "But, I do have resources for homeless – real no sermon help. Temporary places to shower, wash your clothes for free, get food, and maybe some spending money too."

The man she thought was homeless stood there with his head down, his face invisible, his hands behind his back. "Anyway, here's my card. I'm a lawyer in the District Attorney's office. Give me a ring and we'll do what we can to help. Just call and ask for the 'shark'". And Vanessa handed the man she thought was homeless her business card… and in a flash he pounced.

She could only see parts of him in the darkness but she could see there was something in his hands, something that was keeping them from spreading too far apart. A rope? A tie? Maybe, a cord?

Time moved into a special slow-motion gear, like a semi-truck struggling up a steep grade. She could see the man she thought was homeless spring forward with both feet – agile like a frog – to get within arm's reach. She barely had time to get one arm up before his two arms circum-navigated her excellent throat and crossed, leaving the cord tight across her windpipe.

Vanessa had had just enough time to get one finger

under the cord – not enough to keep air flowing to maintain consciousness for long but long enough to gather herself to fight back. She'd had enough training in the ring to remember to think through her move, though her next move wasn't all that creative. It was, however, designed to be devastating.

Vanessa knew it was futile to try to pull backward against a larger opponent and instead pushed forward in a quick jerk, which brought her assailant, who she assumed to be homeless, forward to her, shifting his weight into an awkward and open position. "*Cabron*" she thought. "I was only trying to help, but okay, if he wants to play…." and she let loose a series of vicious and perfectly aimed knees, one after another, right into the groin of the man she assumed to be homeless.

Each hit home perfectly. Each was delivered with enough force to buckle in half a defensive lineman. Four, five, six, knees upward and forward into the area that held the family jewels. Surely, this would bust the jewelry case wide open…

But, the man she presumed to be homeless didn't flinch. Each knee, she realized wasn't hitting the softest part of the human anatomy, smashing them like hacky sacks full of Jello. No, instead, her knees were hitting something hard. Over and over again.

Plastic? PLASTIC?!? What the…

She could feel the cord's grip across her throat, could feel the veins in her neck start to throb, bulge and strain. Her eyes felt like they were bulging too, like tadpoles, but she still had one hand inside the cord and some moments of oxygen left.

The man she assumed was homeless had a curious reek. While some people with bad hygiene cover up their body odor with cologne or perfume, this man was the opposite – he smelled like he was clean underneath some sort of façade of intentional stench.

The sleeves of his course jacket scrapped against her face like rug burn. Underneath the sleeves were well-developed arms – hard, taught biceps ("what kind of homeless man has arms like this?") straining to squeeze the throat, the air, the life out of Vanessa Altuve.

She could hear the rustling of random animals in the bushes. Could smell the dew in the woods from which this violent man emerged. Caught a glimpse of twin headlight eyes watching the silent two-person war that had broken out in the North Royalton Metroparks.

Was that a deer?

Only a brief temptation to panic crossed her mind and then she shifted from self-defense to fighting for her life tactics. Now, it wasn't fighting at all. It was time to attack as an animal!

Already, she realized she was becoming short of breath....started to see spots circling her vision in the Greater Cleveland sky...on a random October night....

7

Leroy Kelly Johnson.

Eddie "the Italian" Johnson (Eddie was no relation. Neither was he Italian).

Bill Combs.

Frank Thomas III.

The four 14-year-old young men stood shoulder pushed against shoulder, like polite commuters might stand in a Tokyo subway. Leroy on the left side facing the street. Eddie "the Italian" on the right. Bill in the middle beside Leroy. Frank in the middle beside Eddie.

It was almost midnight.

Their posture was stilted, almost absurdly erect, like they were standing against a measuring wall straining to be just as tall as they could possibly be. Their chests were also out. Way out. Skinny boys' chests puffed out so much their jeans were loose at the waist. Their jaws were set. Their eyes were wide but determined. They clenched their fists. Together against each others' fists. And down the middle of Murray Hill Road the four conjoined young men began to walk. Slowly. Eyes front. Scared every one of them, but this was a solemn journey. They were walking a path they considered sacred.

A pathway for honor.

For respect.

Eddie "the Italian" grew up hearing stories about Joe Louis from his old man. Grew up hearing stories about Jack Johnson too – America's first Black heavyweight boxing champion. Heard about how the Galveston Giant beat 'em all up – every white man they put in front of him. Heard about how the champ grew rich, dated white women … and then was sentenced to prison for bringing his white girl friend across state lines.

Bill Combs was a good student. Wrote splendid papers about Harriet Tubman, Sojourner Truth, Nelson Mandela, and Malcolm X. Believed the world needed people to stand up for justice – needed Black people willing to suffer for it. When he heard what his friend Leroy planned to do, he couldn't resist the call to stand up himself – to blaze a trail like a new underground railroad down Murray Hill. Ultimately others his color would follow that trail until the wall that stopped Black people from coming down that hill would be torn down once and for all.

And, someone had to take the first steps on that journey.

Frank Thomas III was the only lineman amongst the four Glenville High football players. While the others were lean and wiry, Frank carried a bulky 220 on his 6-foot 2 inch frame – a big kid for the time. He was just there to be with his friends, who were all like his little brothers.

Leroy didn't think about Harriet Tubman or Jack Johnson or Muhammed Ali or Malcolm X. He didn't think about opening doors or blazing trails. He didn't need anyone else to go down this street with him on this day. He only thought that, if he was to become a man, he'd have to stop running someday.

Today would be that day.

It's not hard to spot four African-American young men walking, shoulder to shoulder, heads up with their necks stretching to gain every inch their frames could possibly muster. Not hard to spot even at midnight when you'd think everyone would be sleeping. And, you'd be wrong about that.

It's especially not hard to spot them if they're walking down the middle of the street. And, most of all – most of ALL – it sure isn't hard to spot them if they happen to be walking down the middle of Murray Hill Road in Cleveland's Little Italy.

They didn't walk 30 feet before being spotted by an Ambassador scout. "Hey coon," he whispered to his runner associate around the corner. "Hey coon," he whispered back and ran off.

No, tonight, Leroy's encounter with the Ambassadors wasn't going to be a loud, panicked, disorganized melee. A surprise sprint to the bottom catching the neighborhood off guard. No, tonight, the Ambassadors were prepared. This was what they had planned for, hoped for, wished for... tonight, they were going to defend their neighborhood from invaders in a calm, controlled, composed manner... efficient...ruthless...the way a shark comes after its prey....

The year was 1983.

Jack Wharton was 12.

And invisible.

The call of "Hey coon" in Cleveland's Little Italy quickly and quietly oozed across Murray Hill Road like a dark liquid spilled across the street. It spread like a mad rash from home to home, and each inhabitant hearing the call was stricken with the same fever. "Coons in our neighborhood!"

INVASION!

The Ambassadors organized. Two Tone Tony (because he had a spot of vitiligo on his face) and Joey Pernicano raced with buckets to the back of Pernicano's Authentic Pizza. The East Side Team got the ropes. The West Side Team got the hoods.

Quietly. Quickly. Like mice working in the dark. Mice with a plan. Mice with teeth. Mice morphing into creatures with fangs and no conscience.

Morphing into rats.

Two Tone and Joey returned with their buckets to the part of Murray Hill Road that curved to the southwest. The street lights above had long ago been broken out. By design. Carefully lain design.

Quietly, quickly, the two Italian boys — Two Tone taller

and 16, Joey shorter and squat at 17 — tiptoed out to the middle of the street with their buckets. Quietly, quickly, the two Italian boys – Two Tone wearing jeans and a Black hoody, Joey wearing a beat-up leather jacket – poured the contents of the buckets onto the street, where it oozed from curb to curb like a dark wave covering the beach at night.

The scrap vegetable oil in the buckets, from the barrels behind the family pizzeria, spread like a malignant black ice. Just like the real black ice that would be forming on Cleveland's streets in the winter – the oil was danger-ous… and invisible.

The East Side Team laid their ropes, painted Black, across the Black vegetable oil sheen. The West Side team gave out hoods to each of the three Ambassadors – Dave Acciarri, Joe LaGrecca, and Ray "such a good-looking boy" Cardibello – and made sure the seven "Diplomats" in attendance on this night also had hoods. The clubs, knives, bats, and chains each Italian boy brought on their own.

Each had their preferred way of greeting dark, foreign "guests" to the neighborhood.

In Cleveland's Little Italy.

In 1983.

9

Leroy Kelly Johnson, Eddie "the Italian" Johnson, Bill Combs, and Frank Thomas III continued walking down Murray Hill Road. They remained in locked formation – Leroy on the left side facing the street. Eddie "the Italian" on the right. Bill in the middle beside Leroy. Frank in the middle beside Eddie.

Their pace was slow and methodical, but their hearts were thump, thump, THUMPING along like they were in full sprint. The insides of their fists were getting sweaty, their palms starting to bleed from their nails being clenched tightly, but they couldn't feel anything like pain. All they could feel was their brothers' shoulders pressed against them… and that was enough to keep them moving.

It was quiet. No one was around. They didn't know if that was a good or bad thing.

It felt like a bad thing.

Eddie "the Italian" whispered "maybe, they all asleep." Bill's shoulders untensed just a bit as he let himself admit a strand of hope inside, but Leroy's entire body remained at battle stations. Peering into the darkness. Listening for anything. Was that a cat in the alley to the left? Did he see a shadow to the right? Maybe, someone's dog? Was that whispering or leaves rustling? Sure was dark ahead.

Together, shoulder to shoulder, the four African-American boys from Cleveland's East Side continued their Marco Polo journey into uncharted waters.

"Hey coon."

A whisper from the left.

The four African-American boys hesitated for only a moment until they could all feel Leroy continue striding forward. They were all afraid, and alone, on Murray Hill Road. At night. In the dark. Spotted now.

They kept walking.

"Hey coon," louder this time from the right. They continued but picked up their pace.

"Hey coon! COON!" a loud voice this time from behind – a familiar voice! The voice of the stupid Italian kid who liked to throw rocks.

"Thwok!"

A rock hit Bill right behind his ear, which began bleeding immediately. Bill attempted to turn around, but slipped – slipped to his knees onto the part of the Murray Hill Road that curved to the southwest. The part of Murray Hill Road where the streetlights hadn't worked in a long, long time.

"Hahaha! Strike THREE, coon!" Joe La Grecca – the boy who got "un-enrolled" from Catholic High School, was elated! This was better than Christmas!

"Combs!" Eddie the Italian was shocked to see his nimble friend on the ground, struggling to get to his feet, when – KATHUMP! – he was shocked to realize he was on the ground too! He put his hand on the street – a street that only fractions of a second earlier he had stood atop but which now he fish-flopped around upon himself – and his hand came up… greasy… GREASY?

Something had entangled his legs – something from below that had been pulled taut from opposite ends of the street … causing him to fall. What could be in the middle of the street? Some kind of … ropes?!?

"WHAT THE FUC…!" Bill's voice was cut short by a hood that was strung around his head by two diplomats who waited, barefoot for traction, behind Old Man Macy's truck that never ran.

Frank Thomas III wasn't fast. He wasn't quick. He wasn't particularly smart. But Frank was big. And Frank was faithful. And Frank had big feet, which help when trying to keep your balance standing in the street covered in old vegetable oil from Pernicano's Authentic Pizza.

Frank was able to get just enough traction to throw a big bear's forearm into the nearest Diplomat that had put a hood on his fallen friend. The Diplomat was unconscious before he hit the ground, but then two more came out from behind Mr. Luigi's bushes – the same bushes which just weeks before had provided a thorned place to land for an angry Italian boy who had fallen off his bicycle.

The first of the two reinforcements, barefoot for traction as were all the Italian boys, was greeted for his efforts by a backhand to the cheek from Big Frank, which sent the Diplomat careening to his left, though he was able to keep his feet, just barely. The second boy, using his superior mobility courtesy of his bare feet, scampered around his reeling friend and behind Big Frank.

Big Frank let out a howl, which sounded almost exactly like William Shatner shouting "KHAAAAAN!", and turned to protect his flank from the second attacker who had come from behind the bushes, but the big lineman was too slow and the night, which had been dark, suddenly became pitch black. He couldn't see a thing! He could barely breath!

HOODED!

Leroy and Eddie "the Italian" meanwhile, managed to escape the trap in the slippery street and were standing back to back in front of Mr. Luigi's house. They were soon surrounded by seven Diplomats.

Dave Acciarri, still scabbed and scrapped across his back from his tumble two weeks earlier, had no patience for hoods. He had his special bat. The one he'd so carefully pounded nails into.

He looked. He looked again! Oh happy days! He couldn't believe his luck! The same coon that caused him so much grief only weeks ago. Surrounded in Mr. Luigi's yard! Nowhere to run now. Nowhere to go....

For him, this was better than Christmas too. The Acciarri family didn't have much to give their children for the holidays. Usually, the only gift Dave would remember would be the belt. This was better, for sure. A lot better.

"Well, well, well. If it isn't the coon that likes to run," Dave's grin was the Cheshires' – somehow his only visible part in the dark. "You seem to have taken a wrong turn, boy. We wouldn't be Ambassadors if we didn't try to help" and with that, Dave swung his bat with nails, not at Leroy who he was staring at, but at the legs of Eddie "the Italian" to the young running back's left.

"UHHH!" Eddie felt the weight of the blow first. That was all. That was the scary part. It didn't hurt for a full two seconds…then, wave after wave of intense excruciating pain. Like he had never felt before. It spread and oozed its torturous poison across his leg and he shook and sweat from the intensity of it.

He buckled and tumbled away. And tumbled away. And kept tumbling. And the Ambassadors and the Diplomats stopped paying attention to him as he blended into the shadow in the part of Murray Hill Road that curves Southwest… until he vanished and could no longer be seen. Even on a leg that would turn out to be broken, Eddie "the Italian" ran away.

Leaving Leroy Kelly Johnson alone in Mr. Luigi's front yard.

10

Dave moved on the remaining African-American boy from Cleveland's East Side and swung his bat smartly right at the center of Leroy's torso, but Leroy was too quick again for the angered Ambassador and his bat hit nothing but air. Dave's face wasn't so lucky – Leroy put a RIGHT/LEFT! into the Italian's forehead and left cheek, which sent him to the ground.

Before Leroy could continue his pummeling, however, another boy appeared in front of him. He wasn't much bigger than the others. Not really. He wasn't angrier looking. In fact, he didn't look angry at all. Leroy noticed how nicely his hair was combed.

Ray Cardibello had seen enough of Dave's foolishness with his stupid bat. Ray would show the rest how Ambassadors sign treaties. With their fists. And with their boots.

Without a word, the "good-looking boy" feinted a right, which Leroy reacted to too quickly. He dodged left, only to catch one of the "good-looking boy's" boots into his shin. He hadn't expected that and the damage to his leg left him slowed, off-balance, and feeling vulnerable.

Almost immediately, another kick, a cliché really – a literal boot to the ass – left Leroy stunned – the blow to the nerve center in his buttocks shocked his entire system – he could feel it in his jaw! – leaving his whole body numbed, disconnected, and moving slowly as if in a viscous liquid.

Leroy remembered what he'd brought with him in his pocket.

From the look on Ray's face – that "good-looking face" – no one could ever tell if he were beating someone up or watching the Cleveland Indians winning on the TV.

The same dimples. The same eyes. Black. Deep. Deeper than his dimples. And dark. He was moving in to start directing his kicks to this coon's head. Ray was good with his feet.

Leroy pulled the knife from his pocket. Ray wasn't sure if he saw something shiny or not. He was confident – that "good-looking boy" was confident – and grabbed Leroy by the back of the neck. Leroy stood up, determined to stand tall, and swung out with the knife he'd placed into his pockets what seemed like 10 years ago …

… and the knife had a fated arc…

… a coincidental cause/effect journey like the way washing your car ensures it's going to rain.

From Leroy's lower front right pocket, the knife swung upward and to the left – to the left, right where that good-looking boy had decided to stand, right where the face of that good-looking boy was resting on those good-looking shoulders, and the knife – which wasn't good-looking – swung coincidentally in that dark night on that dark lawn – through the lips of that good-looking boy's face, catching the right corner of that good-look-ing mouth, and continuing beyond the edge of that face creating a long, deep ridge where there wasn't one before.

The knife was sharp.

It finished its journey at the ear of the no longer good-looking boy.

Leroy hardly felt it run its way through the mouth

and cheek of that good-looking boy. Ray hardly felt it himself, but he knew. He knew.

He'd been cut. In the face.

HE'D BEEN CUT! RIGHT IN THE GODDAMN FACE!

By this coon.

THIS MOTHERFUCKING COON!

Two Diplomats behind Leroy didn't see any of this. They just stuck to doing their jobs. They got a hood over the head of Leroy Kelly Johnson. They looked up to see the Lead Ambassador – the one who would never be called good-looking again – press a handkerchief to his face to staunch the bleeding. They saw the look in his eyes change ever so slightly. Only a tad bit darker. Only a tad bit deeper. Like a snake's eyes. A snake about to move on a wounded bird.

And Ray Cardibello, did in fact, move on the hooded African-American youth from Cleveland's East Side.

Young Jack Wharton couldn't sleep that night so he sat out on his porch. In the dark. Watching all of it. Watching every bit of what would happen next.

11

Vanessa Altuve had planned to begin her day with a morning run – the shark cutting through the park. Indestructible. Getting ready for today's courtroom hunt. Getting ready to take down bigger fish. Bigger, rotten fish that needed taking down.

Only this morning, fate would deal her a very bad card.

Now, she was fighting for her life, her umbilical cord to tomorrow held open by the one finger she'd managed to place between her windpipe and this strange homeless-looking man's tightening cord.

She lashed out with everything she had! Kicking shins, stomping feet, reaching for face, reaching for throat, looking, searching in the dark North Royalton morning for eyes to gouge, her head spinning, her spirit roaring – kick and scratch and knee and gouge – her assailant should have been wounded to hospitalization but her every blow hit, not the vulnerable, soft, fleshy parts of the human body that are easily damaged. No, every blow – every single blow – hit something hard instead.

Something that had been … PLANNED.

La Tiburon was feeling herself running out of air, underwater… trapped….

12

Ray Cardibello's big boot kicked upward in a wide sweeping arc. "FLAP!" his boot his the hooded African-American youth's face and made a sound like a hammer hitting a steak. Leroy, the boy within the hood, fell straight backward to the ground. He tried to cover his head with his hands, but then "KUH!" Ray's boot stomped the back of his neck, which made the whole left side of Leroy's body go numb.

Leroy, the boy who could run, was flat on his back unable to move.

FUH, FUH, FUH, FUH…over and over the boots of the once good-looking-boy kicked downward and into the abdomen of the "coon" who had long ago stopped moving. This had already progressed far beyond the beating given to the other captured, hooded boys from Cleveland's East Side – the side where the Black people lived.

FUH, FUH, FUH, FUH, over and over again the stomping continued. Ray's dark eyes still not showing any more emotion than those of a praying mantis attacking a beetle.

The eyes of those around him, however – the other two Ambassadors and the 6 remaining Diplomats – those eyes told a different story. A sad story. A helpless story. A story of being witness to something they wished wasn't happening, but that it wasn't any of their places to try to stop.

To even say a word.

The eyes of a small, non-Italian boy on the porch nearby, peering from the dark, were silent too.

13

Vanessa Altuve, the attorney who fought for justice, the one called La Tiburon, "the shark", felt herself weakening. Her fighting spirit continued to command her limbs to fight – to kick, and scratch, and punch and grab – but her body's ability to obey those commands waned – each blow now less forceful than the previous.

And still, this strange man who'd attacked her in the Metroparks, the one she'd stopped to help, continued to squeeze on the cord that choked her, that stole her breath in an attempt to steal her life. The single finger she'd managed to shove in between the killing cord and her windpipe not enough to provide the air she needed to stay alive.

She continued flailing but her one arm and legs now moved only softly and randomly, like a sock puppet hung by a string blowing in the wind.

She thought of the day she'd planned – a day spent fighting for a cause. Who would pick up that cause now? She thought of the life she might have lived – a life that wasn't that of a solitary hunter. A life not in battle against the forces that exploit the weak – that took advantage of people they felt weren't as important as profit. Forces that didn't care if her poor papa would work himself to death.

She thought of this alternate life – the one she might have lived – the one that wasn't solitary – wasn't focused on a life mission.

Wasn't alone.

As the world grew fuzzier and fuzzier around the edges … and not having air to breathe became something she was somehow growing comfortable with … she imagined herself living as *una esposa, una madre*, in a simple village.

She imagined herself fat, not someone who runs down the parkway. Surrounded by children, lots of children, some of the *ninos* scraped and dirty from playing outside as boys should play. Some of the *ninas* helping their mama make tortillas.

Wearing a flowing dress… in the kitchen…

She thought of her papa and – what?

There.

A Glow.

An image.

She saw him now! Saw that loving face. That heart of his. That strength.

What?

She could could…hear him.

She could hear his voice. *"Como hacéis al menos de estos…."*.

She could hear him say

"Entonces tú me lo hiciste" she could hear herself reply. And she knew that her father understood how she had dedicated her life to living those words. She could feel the enormous pride her father felt in her daughter. She could see her father stretch out her hands.

And, she walked forward to embrace him.

14

Leroy Kelly Johnson could always run. Was gifted that way. Could never be caught by behind.

But, on this day, he had chosen not to run. Had chosen to stand and fight a fight he couldn't win. Now, he couldn't run. Hooded and broken, he laid on the ground helpless and felt the invisible blows – at first, the pain was staggering – powerful, intense, as though his whole body were nothing but pain.

Gradually, however, he could only feel pressure. No pain. Just pressure, the way a drilled tooth feels under Novocain. He knew he was being struck. Struck HARD. But, it was as though it was someone else's body. Something disconnected from him.

He managed to move. He managed to stick out his chest.

He managed to make that one final defiant gesture. No matter what, no one could take away from him his successful journey, as a young Black man, down Murray Hill Road. Alone. No matter what, no one could take away from him his returning a second time… and refusing to run.

The hood no longer kept him in darkness. Somehow, the night was filled with light. A very bright light. He felt himself moving to that light. He felt himself running to that light. Fluid and free, like a bird flying.

His strides were… beautiful.

And free.

And proud.

Like a king, but no…a prince.

Toward the end zone.

And only he would know if he managed to run across the goal line.

…this was the day Jack Wharton decided to become a cop.

15

The Other looked down at the dead woman he'd just strangled. He was surprised by how hard she had fought, but that didn't matter. He'd prepared as only someone with his training would prepare. He still had work to do with this fallen warrior, however. That was also according to plan.

According to long-lain plans.

After, after he finished here, he would wend his way back through the dark woods, seen only by the deer that some felt grew like vermin in the neighborhoods, like rats. He would get into the car he'd hidden. Drive to the location he'd chosen. Take off his soiled, smelly, clothing. Take off his motorcycle jacket. Take off the shin guards, the athletic cup, the hard-plastic mask protecting his face. Take off the all the customized battle armor. He'd dispose of it all exactly as he'd planned. Until, next time.

But, for now, he still had work to do.

When he was finished here, he would turn to the path in the woods.

And whisper.

"The Other is the Other," said the Other. "That is all."

When he was finished here, he would turn to the path in the woods.

And whisper.

"The Other is the Other," said the Other. "And, that is all."

"<u>Not a Poem</u>

I used to write poetry.

I really did.

I used to write poems.

I really did."

This is what John Wharton looked at every morning as he shaved. It was written in a child's handwriting taped to his mirror. He had written it a long time ago. He wasn't sure why he liked it so much. He just did.

Taped to the other corner of the mirror was another poem – one he'd seen written once on a bathroom wall.

"I saw a man upon a stair.

I saw a man who wasn't there.

I saw that man again today.

Gee, I wish he'd go away."

That poem was typed years ago on a typewriter. He didn't know why he liked that one either. He just did. He shaved off his overnight stubble and rinsed the razor in the sink. As always, he was up at 5 am. As always, sleep had been fitful and filled with forgotten bits of dreams. How could he know that only a half hour earlier a young woman was fighting a losing battle for her life only five miles away in the North Royalton Metroparks?

"*I am Iron Man!*" his phone was ringing. A call this early had to be from his partner, the guy he called his silent partner.

"Yallo"

"Hey Jack, we got a customer". The familiar voice of his partner, the guy he just called "Johnson."

"Ok, Johnson, what we got?"

"Well, it won't be donuts first thing this morning, I'm afraid" and Jack could sense Johnson's grin over the phone. Johnson had been a homicide detective, and Jack's erstwhile partner, for many years. Maybe too many. He was a solid investigator. Also, a creep.

"Ok"

"Looks like we got psycho. Strangulation on the Metroparks with some etcetera. Some creative etcetera"

"Ok, location?"

"We're setting up shop at Aukerman Park, off York Road by Valley Parkway. And Jack, I know your tummy. You probably want to eat some breakfast first."

"Be there in 15 minutes"

"Oh, and one more thing. She's an attorney at the District's Attorney's office. Spanish chick named Vanessa Al Toov"

Jack finished shaving. Stared in the mirror. Thought about the victim, who he'd heard about. Passed her in the courtroom halls, he was pretty sure. Pretty. Firm.

Intense. Stood tall. Walked with long strides. Long brown hair.

Thought of how precious life is. Thought about how fragile it's hold. Thought about his job. The one he thought would help him change the world. Now, it just kept sending him into life's dumpster to pull out the worst shit.

"Fuck"

Cut himself.

Wiped off. Finished getting dressed. Quick shot of Fireball, which tasted and smelled like his toothpaste.

Time for Jack Wharton to get to work.

17

Sargent Detective Jack Wharton drove his 2004 Ford Explorer into the macabre pageantry that had become his life's work. Pulling into Aukerman Park under a grey Cleveland blanket felt like cruising a carnival midway outside what they used to call a "Freak Show "– flashing lights, yellow tape, crowds of people milling about, some with tense expressions, others looking shocked. Random shouts, murmurs, voices, mystery.

He saw his partner wave him over.

"This one's creative, got to hand it to him. He likes to write." The guy he called Johnson explained as he leaned over the open driver window. Jack just nodded, indicating he was going to park.

"I've already seen this guy's work. I'll just sit in your car and write up my report while you can go over and get caught up," and Johnson got into the Explorer on the passenger side and started fumbling with his tablet. He never spoke with the brass or most anyone other than his partner. That's how he worked.

Police cars were spread around the area like a child's toys – scattered randomly on shoulders of the road, driveways, grassy fields, and every which way they could find a corner to rest. Jack started noting things on his phone's memo pad – time, location, general impressions – as he walked up to center stage… to the oblong shape under a sheet surrounded by another perimeter of yellow tape.

Photographers, investigators, and various random people whose time and place at this time and place made this part of their lives. A part of their lives today and now they had a hard time believing was real… and a part they'd always wish in vain they could cut out.

"Wharton!"

Holy Crap! Was that the Chief of Police? Part of an early-morning, on-scene, initial investigation? This was a first…. "Wharton, I'd like you see this. Get your take." Calvin D. Williams was the City of Cleveland's 40th Chief of Police. Appointed to the Division of Police on February 24, 1986, and a former head of the city's SWAT team. He wasn't a former badass. His badassery was present tense, and if he called someone over, they generally came… pronto.

"Yessir, Chief" and Wharton ducked under the inner-most tape fence and approached the centerpiece of this flashing lights show. Chief Williams lifted the sheet.

It was like looking at a Dali painting – surreal to the point where a human brain takes some time to digest it all, to come to understand the unprecedented visuals its eyes were reporting and to strain to interpret what it meant. Even here like this, he could tell this was the striking, bold-striding young attorney he'd seen before in the courthouse halls.

She'd been strangled, that much was obvious. Her throat was cut and bruised and her neck was at a strange angle. Her skin had a bluish hue from a lack of oxygen. Her body, however, hadn't been left so much as it was positioned – arranged in a deliberate pose. She was left flat on her back with her legs spread out at the knees but then her feet joining at the bottom, like someone might look when clicking their heels.

Her right hand was left with her pointy finger stuck under her chin, as in a demure expression. Her eyes had been taped open, and her mouth had been taped upward at the edges as though to suggest… a smile?

Her left arm was straight out, and … missing a finger?

Jack Wharton looked at this once-attorney, who he'd known by reputation as a crusader. He looked at her like a mechanic might scan the engine of a car that wasn't running right, his mind clicking through a checklist of items to be trouble-shot.

She was wearing running gear and headphones. Was she in the habit of running alone this early in the morning? No reason not to – this area is "considered safe" – but if this run were part of her routine, the attack might not have been random. Someone who carried a grudge from a previous case perhaps?

No, this wasn't likely to be a grudge. This was sick. This wasn't someone who was angry. This was someone who was operating under another reality – a reality where empathy and compassion were just illusions – performance art to disarm the next potential victim.

She'd been left on the ground looking like a busted puppet on a broken string.

Jack looked next in the direction of the pointing arm. The Chief gently put the drape back down atop what had been Vanessa Altuve and motioned Jack in that direction. Six feet from the body there was a message written onto the pathway.

Three words.

"Fear the Other". They'd been written in blood.

Vanessa Altuve's blood.

The Chief pointed to something else – something cylindrical around 2 inches long, with what looked like paint on one tip and what looked like blood covering the other.

The missing finger.

"We believe this is what the killer used to write this message. Make any sense to you?"

"The Other? The other what?"

"That's what we have to figure out. Wharton, you know this is about our family now, right? She wasn't a cop, exactly, but she was one of us working to catch the bad guys. More than that, she'd caught the attention of the right people in Columbus. Jack, people were talking about her someday becoming Senator. If she were the goddamn president, we wouldn't… we wouldn't…." and the badass Chief turned and walked away. A morning misty drizzle began to fall in the North Royalton Metroparks. It fell across the area wetting the windows all around giving the flashing lights a speckled aura. It fell on the face of the badass Chief.

Jack would soon be getting reports filed through email and posted on the department's secure internal wiki. He'd participate in brainstorm discussion groups creating a profile of the killer. But, Jack knew that this madman (and it almost definitely was a man) was almost certainly not going to be stopped until he had killed again.

18

"Hey Jack, come over here." Dick Mulvaney, one of the officers who'd been interviewing a shaken youth near the corpse, called the Sargent Detective over. "Ok, son, nice and easy… here wipe your nose…tell this man here exactly what you told me."

"I never, I never…never wanted to, to…" the 13-year-old began to stammer.

"Deep breath, son" Wharton held a handkerchief so the boy could blow his nose.

"I never wanted to see anyone get hurt. Ever. Like this" he tried to continue. "But, my folks say I need to be responsible, they told me, and to be responsible I had to earn my own money."

"Okay, son, that's good that your parents would tell you that. Mine told me the same thing," Jack was telling the truth. "Where are your parents now?"

"Mom should be here any minute." Mulvaney answered for the boy. "Dad's at work, but he'll be here shortly."

"Ok, good. See, your parents will be here soon" Jack reassured the shaken youth, "That will make you feel better."

The boy's reaction was not as Jack expected, however. "Don't patronize me, officer. It's going to be a long time, a long fucking time before I feel better about this." The boy seemed to find strength in his own swearing. "Sorry, sir, but I've just never dealt with seeing a dead person before."

"What's your name, boy?"

"Eduardo Espinosa. I live on Nottingham Parkway."

"Ok, Eduardo, tell us what happened."

"Well, I get up early to pick up the Cleveland Plain Dealer for my paper route. The papers are left in a bundle about half a mile from here at 4 am. I ride my bike to pick them up and then deliver them in my neighborhood."

"That's awfully early"

"You're telling me, but that's how I got my bicycle. And, I'm supposed to be saving for college."

"Ok, so you came by to get your papers – about what time was that?"

"It was little before 4 am, uh, Mr….."

"Wharton. Officer Wharton, but you can call me Sarg'"

"Ok, well, uh, Sarg', I come riding up from around the corner there, and I think I see somebody moving around over here, which is odd because I hardly never see anybody up that early. I'm thinking maybe it's a homeless guy or even maybe a deer…or maybe just the guy I saw out here yesterday… "

"You saw a man here yesterday?" Wharton interrupted.

"Yessir. Got a real good look at him too."

"Ok, you saw him yesterday. Was it around the same time?"

"Uh huh" and Eduardo wiped his nose. "Do you think he's the guy that done this, done this.. (sob) to this lady?"

"Well, that's what we'll try to find out, young man. Please, continue."

"So, anyway, this man was out here yesterday morning

about this same time and there was just something about him that didn't seem right. He was looking around, kinda' sneaky like, and going through the trash. I figured he was homeless or something. But, I was on my bike, so I rode past him, just to see him, and he gave me this hard look. Like someone who wanted to start a fight."

"And, if you saw this man again, could you recognize him?"

"Oh, for sure!"

"How can you be sure?"

"Because he had a mark or something on his right cheek. It went nearly to his ear. I'd never forget that. It looked like he always was smiling out of that side of his face."

Sargent Wharton felt a vague recollection which he couldn't place, but his infamous stomach started to percolate a bit.

"Ok, and then what?"

"I just rode off real fast to deliver my papers."

"And that was yesterday."

"Uh huh."

"What happened this morning?"

"Like I said, I went to pick up my papers, saw something moving in the dark over here, and figured maybe it was the same guy. So, I really didn't even look over. I just went and got my papers. On my way back, I rode by, and saw something lying here, and thought maybe a deer got hit by a car, and then I, then I… oh God, oh God! Oh Gooooooood! Nooooo!"

Officer Mulvaney put a strong arm around the distraught youth just as his mother pulled into the parking lot. Wharton went back over to the body. Thought about other broken bodies he'd seen. Thought about a guy with a scar on his right cheek. A memory teased him but wouldn't land. But, the teasing was enough.

"Guys with scars on their right cheek…"

19

PROSECUTING ATTORNEY SLAIN, No Motive or Suspect in Early Morning Metroparks Strangulation

Jack Wharton put down the front page of the Cleveland Plain Dealer. "You know pard'ner, the local paper exploiting this isn't the worst of it. That whole newspaper industry is going the way of Leave it to Beaver. The local television news crews seemed to at least try to remember this was a beautiful young woman who'd had her life snuffed out by some sicko. But, the national media just turn my stomach. What are they calling him? The Sherwood Forest assassin? That's some sick shit right there too. Like this son of a bitch is fucking Robin Hood."

Jack's gulp left only one finger of Jack Daniels remaining from the three he'd poured into his glass.

"Tell ya' what, Wart, that Altuve was some looker," his partner, Johnson, gave a whistle. "Those national folks just love to put those hot Mexican chicks on the air. Good for ratings. They called her the shark, but I think she was more of an electric eel. Zzzzzzt. Arirba!"

Jack had long since learned to ignore his partner's coarseness, which most found offensive, and given up on trying to clean up his act. It was why they were part-nered – Jack was one of the few people who could stand the guy.

But, at the end of the day, Johnson was a top-notch investigator – a chemistry major with minors in foren-sics and statistics – capable of performing magic in the remarkable home crime lab that took up most of their shared living space in the two-bedroom apartment they called home.

Even if he was a bigoted asshole.

"Yah. Arriba."

Jack stared out the window. Stared out from their subur-ban home office in Berea, the place Johnson called their "Berea Batcave." Looked out at the stark grey trees whose branches were clinging to the final straggling dull brown leaves that had, only weeks earlier, been rainbows across the horizon.

Looked out at the grey pavement, the grey sky, the grey intermittent drizzle, the grey neighboring buildings, the grey clouds, the grey air enveloping his grey world. A dismal, limp, orange pumpkin-shaped bag full of leaves wandered about his front yard in the breeze… staggering a few feet this way, a few feet that way, as though intentionally keeping itself within a little 3 foot circle boundaried by an invisible fence. He turned away from the pumpkin bag meandering drunkenly around his front yard, going nowhere.

"Okay, let's do this again. Where were we?"

"Ok, Wart, here's our pretty puzzle. Brilliant, dynamic, badass broad. Goes for her early morning run. By the evidence on the ground, it looks like some nutter sitting fairly still in the dark, boozing it up by himself, spilling his hooch all around. As she runs by, he pops out, there's a violent fight, and he strangles her to death with some cord or garrote, which he just happens to be carrying in his pocket as he's just sitting there in woods. Then, he leaves some kind of message in the victim's blood on the sidewalk, walks back into the woods, and vanishes, without leaving any useful DNA evidence. That about the size of it?" Johnson reached for another Bud Light.

"Give me the forensics on her remains, again?"

"Sure, Wart. Mostly, we got a brown fox turned Black and blue. Deep bruising from head to toe. Bruises on the top of her knees, her elbows, her fists, and… two busted knuckles on her right hand. And, of course, the detached finger paint brush. The coroner has a theory that whatever was used to choke her also detached her finger, like she got it stuck on it somehow. That's about it. Oh yeah. And the word 'other' engraved on her chest. What's that sound like to you?"

"Like a puzzle with pieces that don't fit. You ever see

Vanessa in the ring, Johnson?"

"Can't say I have."

"She regularly did Muy Tai rounds with men. If she tried, she could have gone pro − I'm talking MMA. These nutjobs usually don't take on anyone that tough, let alone manage to kill them. Who is this guy?"

"You're suggesting training?"

"Has to be some kind of training. Maybe military. And another thing. You get the report about her nails?"

"Let's see." Johnson had the coroners report on one of the several monitors on the various desks in their Batcave. "Searching nails… here you go. All ten nails cracked and broken… no DNA beneath. Your point?"

"I've seen the Shark fight. I don't care who she's fighting. That woman was going to draw blood. Couple times in court, she looked at me like a rabid cat and I could feel my skin ready to be torn just from her looking at me. How could she be fighting the battle of the century, with all that bruising from throwing blows, and not draw a single skin cell under a nail? What the hell happened out there?"

"That's why they pay us the small buck, Wart". Johnson threw his empty at the basketball hoop over the waste basket. It clanked off the backboard and bounced onto the floor. Alongside the others. Johnson grabbed another Bud from the cooler.

"So, we got a crazy who's also a badass. Course, I'm not ruling out premeditation. Could be premeditated made to look random nut. That's the direction the chief is leaning toward."

"I dunno', Johnson. Doesn't feel like a fake crazy guy. Doesn't feel like anything right now. I can't make the puzzle pieces fit. A random nut not typically this careful in the planning. Someone trying to pretend to be crazy… not usually this good at it. I just know this is a very dangerous guy, and we don't have shit right now to go on."

Jack Wharton felt like he was holding time in his gut – like existence itself were somehow a delicately constructed Christmas tree ornament that might shatter if he so much as stopped paying attention to it. Somewhere inside his instincts told him a boundary had been crossed, that something that had been keeping things together had cracked, and now the dam had broken… and there weren't enough king's horses and king's men to put it back together again. It felt like he hadn't taken a really deep breath in a long, long time.

"We got one thing. That kid that saw the guy with the scar. What time's he due at the office?"

Johnson looked at his watch. "Right now."

"Let's roll, pard'ner. We got a super villain to catch."

"Come on, Wart. You know I never go the office. I'll keep working angles here and you let me know what you find out."

The cop who was called "Wart" by his partner, and his partner only, put on his Cleveland Browns jacket, his

Black winter hat, popped some gum into his mouth, and walked out into a drizzly Cleveland afternoon. It was the day before Halloween.

20

Eduardo Espinosa, the young man from Nottingham Parkway in the tony Cleveland suburb of North Royalton, had seen better days. Just two days ago, he was upset that his girlfriend didn't answer his text and he had gotten jealous. That was the major cloud in his life… two days ago.

Today, he was living a bad dream he couldn't wake up from. This part of his dream had him sitting in a police station with his parents in a meeting room with no windows. They were sitting on drab, worn, brown leather meeting chairs – the type of good office furniture public agencies buy when they get a budget and then have to continue using far beyond their expected useful life. They were comfortably conformed to fit an infinite number of butts that had each left their unique imprints over the years.

Also in the room were a man and a woman. The man was Chief Inspector Tim Sobolewski, a ruddy man with a broad chest who was in his mid-50s, but looked older. The woman was tall and thin, with bony features and sharp-looking eyebrows and elbows. She introduced herself as "Dr. Stephanie Woodward". Dr. Woodward was a Social Worker specializing in working with children who had experienced trauma, but Eduardo mostly noticed her warm eyes that peered from behind glasses on that bony nose from what seemed like the ceiling. Dr. Woodward's skeletal frame and long limbs made her 5'11" height seem even taller.

Eduardo sat at a chair near the front of the table facing a projector. His mother, Mary Isabelle Espinosa, sat in the chair next to his. Her dark eyes showed only traces of remaining evidence of the tears she'd been crying. Instead, a deep well of maternal strength seemed to radiate from her, emotionally cocooning her boy in a protective bubble from her heart. She was short and round, but right now, seemed like the biggest person in the room to her son. She held her son's hand firmly, held her head high, and looked everyone there square in the face. This was her son. She was there for her son.

In the chair across from Eduardo sat his father, Adrian Guillermo Alejandro Espinosa. Adrian was a bricklayer, and his friends just called him "Brick". Although today he was "Mr. Espinosa." He was calloused from head to toe and even had the shape and coloring of a brick. He had shed many tears overnight that no one had seen. There was no evidence of any of that today on his face. Today, he looked like a Lucha Libra wrestler, unmasked, sitting out of place in an office room. He was there for his son, too, and his presence was that of a quiet, humble, respectful bouncer.

On the projector, a series of photographs and drawings were being shown. The pictures were of known suspects who had scars on their faces. The drawings were composite artist's renderings from Eduardo's description. The drawings and the photographs were intermittently exchanged as additional changes to the drawing would be made as Eduardo pointed out features from the photographs that matched the "person of interest" he had seen in the park.

Jack Wharton walked in from a door in the back with the practiced invisibility of an experienced undercover cop. Nonetheless, Eduardo had his senses shocked into primal mode and he turned around in response to even the quietest footfall.

"Morning, Sarge" Eduardo tried to sound upbeat, but his every sentence sounded like he was fighting back tears. If only he could get that image out of his head….

Jack just nodded, retreating into invisibility in the back, and Eduardo got back to work.

"Nope. Not that one. The guy I saw wasn't Black" he continued. "Not that one either, the guy I saw was darker than that, more like me than like Mr. 'Sulbeski' here. Ok, his chin was kinda' like this guy's – maybe we can have the drawing shaped more like this guy's chin? Not him either…."

"How's it going?" Jack whispered to Inspector Sobolewski, who today was happy with "Sulbeski". He'd been called worse.

"So far, no good. You know how many inmates, creeps, weirdos, parolees, ex-cons, and scumbags have a scar on their right cheek?"

Jack shrugged.

"One thousand, seven hundred and twenty-two in our data base alone, and that's not even integrating the Feds' data! We got a long way to go and I'm not even sure we can trust this kid. You know Mexicans."

Jack looked over at the Espinosas. He trusted them.

A face appeared on the projector and Jack's world faded away. The words of those around him blurred into a formless sound mush as everyone's syllables blended into a bland, meaningless background slow-motion soup. He felt like someone who had been searching for a word all day long – longer! – and had just heard, not THE word, but a word something like it.

He was looking at a face. A swarthy, olive-skinned face with a scar across the right cheek. And it wasn't THE person who his memory struggled to find – no, that was just outside his grasp like a searched for, hidden word on the tip of his tongue – letting him know it's there, but not letting him grasp it, like a mosquito buzzing in the dark.

But, it was close enough to remind him. There was something important in his memory that he needed to find. He sat there, with Inspector Sulbeski today, with the tall, skeletal Social Worker with the warm eyes and scarecrow build, with Mr. and Mrs. Espinosa, with the traumatized boy who understood his own healing would have to wait … and watched image after image appear on the screen, trying to find that mosquito memory teasing him in the dark.

21

"Everyone dies the same. Everyone's blood is red. If it takes fear to bring us to understand that – if the streets need to run red to bring us together – to stop hating each OTHER over our differences – then the Other will be the last other and bring us together … by opening up our secret innards and paint those streets red… red that will run … together."

Jack Wharton read the note again, aloud to his partner, Johnson.

"Welp. That's pretty crazy" his long-time partner laughed. "You think it's legit?"

"I don't know. I don't know what to think. Could be from anybody," Jack replied. "Just something in my gut tells me it could be our man."

"And, it was mailed to you? Here, in the Batcave?"

"Yeah, that's another thing that's spooky about it."

"A nutter might get your name from the paper, but it's not easy finding a cop's home address. If this is our boy, he's a very special kind of crazy," Johnson lit a cigarette and let a plume fill the room.

"I'm taking it to the office now. Have the professor look at it. Wanna' come?"

Johnson grabbed a Bud Lite. "Can't. Been drinking. Would only make you look bad."

22

"See the big red capital 'O' in 'Other' written on the bottom?" asked the examiner they called "the Professor."

"You mean the one that looks like it was made by a frustrated graphic designer?" Jack answered the Professor, who didn't like having his questions answered with questions.

"You know what that's written with?"

The question answered itself. Jack frowned.

"It's type AB+. You know what percentage of Latino-Americans are type AB+?" the Professor like asking questions. Jack was in no mood to play student, but he was surprised he hadn't even considered what type of ink was on his anonymous letter.

"Two percent. You know who else is AB+? I mean was?" The professor didn't wait for a response this time. "Our late, lovely, murdered Assistant District Attorney, Vanessa Altuve. We won't have DNA for another 24 hours, Jack, but it's highly likely he used her blood to write that letter on this note."

Jack stared at the note, which had just changed in his own mind from some crackpot's sick joke to something reverent, like a holy church relic.

Neil Kendricks-Johnson, aka the Professor, was generally considered a genius in police circles. Six foot, four inches with broad shoulders and a large head, a broad nose, full lips, and big feet, he was darker than his African-American dad and, of course, his Caucasian mother. For reasons known only to Neil, he wore his hair in a Jheri-curl.

He looked, at first glance, like an out-of-shape defensive tackle, though he hated sports and never worked out a day in his life. In truth, he was as physically un-gifted as any of his fellow Syracuse University nerds, but no one ever believed it. The Professor looked for all the world like the typical "big scary Black guy" that skittish white women cross the street to avoid. He also happened to be a world-renowned forensic scientist who combined encyclopedic knowledge with unique observational skills and ESP-like instincts. No one else would have thought to examine the red ink on a crackpot note. That's why he was the Professor.

"Unless the DNA says otherwise, and I don't think it will, this is your boy, all right. And this is one helluva' bad puppy. He planned this out like the storming of Normandy, right down to bringing home enough blood to write that letter. You'll need to talk to the psychological forensic guys to profile this guy, but from what little I know, you've got that rare predator who actually believes he's fighting for a cause." The Professor paused to look out the window as though he were searching, scanning the horizon imagining how difficult it is to find one man who is just out there... somewhere.

"Jack, guys like this don't see the people they kill as victims. They see them as casualties. Unfortunate casualties of a greater war. Collateral damage. And they are heroes in their own story. Makes him not a monster. Not in his own mind, anyway. Makes him a crusader, a liberator. Like the French Underground blowing up train stations. Opposing evil."

The Professor was lecturing, but that's what people do sometimes when they are the smartest person in the room, any room. "But, of course, you'll want to talk to the psych' team. I'm not really an expert in this area."

"Why now, Prof'?" Jack's question brought the Professor's gaze back into the room. "Where did this guy come from? You gonna' give me one of those 'he didn't get breast fed enough from his mama' lines?"

"Yes. That's exactly my layman's theory to this point. People like this are broken early as children. Something bad happened, some trauma, and it just sits there waiting, waiting, for a trigger. Something years and years later that tears open the wound that never healed, rips off the scab and what comes out," the Professor resumed his searching gaze out the window. "What comes out is all the poison that's been festering all those years, down below.

"The Other is real, Jack. He's out. He believes he's in some kind of grand war. He's clever. Real clever."

"And it's my job to stop him. And all we got is it 'might' be a guy with a scar on his face. Lovely."

Jack walked out the door, down the drive that had been the target of the Professor's gaze, to his car. He opened the door and paused to look around at the surrounding

MetroParks, a place that, until recently, was considered safe.

23

Jack Wharton was a fish. Most of the time. Sometimes, he was a child in a bed that had, long ago, been left to rot in a landfill, but most of the time a fish. Jack, as both a fish and as a child, was always in a fishbowl – a fishbowl surrounded by bigger fish – fish with fangs and names. Jack, as both a fish and a child, watched the fish outside his bowl cut and tear at other fish, fish that were different, and he remained motionless in his bowl to try to be unnoticed.

Sometimes, a fish would stare menacingly inward, to glare at Jack, to mock the one in the fishbowl, who was, like the others they would feast upon…different. And then, the surrounding fish, would wander off.

Was he friends with the fish outside, the ones who were tearing at the others? He wasn't sure. He only knew he had to remain very still, in that fishbowl which some-times was his childhood bed, but usually wasn't.

Very, very still.

Finally, one big fish stared at him most menacingly. This fish was like those who did the tearing, but was different too. Different in the way it looked, different in the way "he" looked, he thought. This fish had a very different smile – a smile that was crooked – a smile that was very,

very long on the right side – so long, in fact, it went all the way to the top of his head…and, Jack became very, very afraid. Afraid of the fish staring at him, not with anger or hatred, no – staring at him with something much scarier than that.

This one, this fish with the crooked smile, this one looked at Jack…with indifference…like the way a snake looks at a nest full of eggs before swallowing them … as indifferent to the snuffing of emerging life as gazing at a silent moon…and Jack woke up with his heart pounding!

Racing like he had been sprinting up a steep staircase and not just lying in his bed, his bed in Berea, Ohio. Breathing heavily like he'd been punching a heavy bag instead of sleeping in his bed at home … and the image of the different fish came immediately to mind, the fish with that crooked smile … and he remembered.

He remembered!

He found the thought that had been teasing him from the outskirts of his recollection since he'd heard the boy talk about the man he'd seen the morning of the murder – it was like remembering the name of your favorite actor that you couldn't find all day, and suddenly, it was there.

The name.

"Ray Cardibello" he whispered into the dark, still panting for breath. "The Ambassadors' biggest fish. Ray fucking Cardibello!"

24

The Other was invisible in plain site again. He looked homeless – filthy, thrift store clothes, baggy in the rear, mismatched, torn with holes, speckled with dark blotches which, one supposed, were the results of random bodily fluids indifferently allowed to accessorize his look. And, of course, he reeked like a Port-a-Loo that had long since needed maintenance. Tattered, tortured-looking "Make America Great Again" hat down low over his eyes, with a piece of cardboard glued and stapled to the brim to extend it… the sort of random clothing modification homeless people do, for random reasons, known only to them. Their unique personalization of the garbage they call clothes. The cardboard stuck out a good six inches beyond the end of the brim. Written on the extension piece with black marker were two words, "spare change".

The Other's costume today for the role he was to play.

His uniform today for the war he believed he was fighting.

Camouflaged today.

For what he was to do today.

"Game time. Game Face" he thought.

He staggered through the Tower City Rapid Station, underground in downtown Cleveland. Located at 50 Public Square, the station, according to the City of Cleveland Regional Transit Authority website is "the busy hub of RTA's rail network. All rail lines converge here, and many RTA bus routes serve the area near the Station."

The 1,000-foot Walkway to Gateway, built and operated by RTA, connects Tower City to Quicken Loans Arena, home to the National Basketball Association Cleveland Cavaliers, the American Hockey League Cleveland Monsters, and the Arena Football League Cleveland Gladiators. Nearby, Tower City Center, Horseshoe Casino Cleveland, and the Ritz-Carlton Hotel are better all attractions than most people would expect when they think of downtown Cleveland. Exactly one mile away is the Rock n' Roll Hall of Fame.

The Other looked around. He saw the binary diversity that is Cleveland, a demographic schizophrenic city with white people living on one side, the West, and Black people living on the other side, the East. Some West-side suburban communities, like Parma, Brunswick, and North Royalton, are 97% white. East side communities are the opposite – Warrensville Heights, for example, is over 90% Black.

Here, beneath Cleveland's downtown Public Square, the Other saw a place where these two different worlds, east and west, meet – a rare common ground of community color with roughly a 50/50 mix in white and Black passersby. Although Cleveland, like all of America, has robust communities of every race and ethnicity, when he looked around from his role play of homeless man, he mostly saw white faces and Black faces, walking past each other, usually without eye contact or acknowledgement.

He, himself, was also immune to any eye contact. Passersby treated him as though his homelessness were contagious by sight – as though just looking at him might cause them to become like him… disgusting. A barnacle person. One to be shunned. Those who would dare a peek at him would do so the way someone looks at a solar eclipse – hurriedly, out of the corner of their eye for only a brief fraction of a second. To look at him any longer would mean accepting that he is a human, and therefore meriting more than indifference. To stare – to really look – at him meant that you might find it appropriate… to care.

Thinking of that…The Other smiled ….

An estimated 30,000 persons a day use this station. The Other thought to himself, as he carried his reek in a stumbling meander alongside the tracks, some of them would be using this station for the last time.

25

"That's it! That's him! The man in the park! *Dios mio!* That's the man!" Eduardo Espinosa put his head down in his hands and cried into his mother's arms – the honest arms she had wrapped around him the moment she saw the look of recognition on her *hijo's* face. "That's him! That's him! The man I saw! That morning. Mom! Mom! There he is," wailed the slender Mexican youth through his sobs. Eduardo's father, Adrian Guillermo Alejandro Espinosa, quietly stood up and put his strong, calloused, honest bricklayer's hands gently on his wife's shoulders.

Jack Wharton looked over at Chief Inspector Tim Sobolewski, whose face muscles seemed to unflex for the first time in a week. Dr. Stephanie Woodward, the Social Worker assigned to support their young witness, professionally strode over to the family and professionally stood near them, her presence providing a physical sense of support, a caring psychic blanket, even though she wasn't touching any of them.

Wharton and Sobolewski nodded and quietly walked out into the hall.

"You say you know this guy, Jack?" The Chief Inspector wasn't a believer in coincidences, and so was skeptical when Sargant Wharton suggested he might know the man they were looking for – the man the boy in the room had seen in the Metroparks the morning of Vanessa Altuve's murder.

"Just a kid I knew in the neighborhood I grew up in. I remember he had some sort of accident that left him with a nasty scar on his right cheek. Lost touch when I graduated high school and went into the Navy." Jack looked out the window and spoke as though he were recounting a dream.

"I remember he was a violent troublemaker, even as a kid. I'd heard that, after his accident, things went down-hill. He spent a lot of short terms in the stir for the usual

– protection racket, dealing, and pimping mostly." Jack woke up now and looked at the Chief Inspector straight in the eye. "A natural predator. Probably a sociopath. He's a dangerous human being, a misfit, Tim, right out of the womb...."

"And, guys like that usually end up on the street, going through garbage cans in the Metroparks when normal people are sleeping," the Chief Inspector finished Jack's thought. "Well, I have no doubt that's who the kid saw. But, what made you think of him?"

"Just a hunch, Tim. You know a good cop has to trust his hunches." Jack made something that almost resembled a smile for the first time in what felt like a long time.

Inspector Sobolewski didn't believe in hunches either, but however it came about, they now had a "person of interest" the entire force would be motivated – highly motivated – to find and bring in. A homeless guy with a scar named Ray Cardibello.

The Other half-stumbled like a man in his own personal earthquake trying to keep his feet, and half-shuffled, like a zombie. All around him, the mainstreamers were living their mainstream lives. Most bustled about with a sense of purpose – people with jobs, and responsibilities – people on a schedule whose watches always seemed to have bad news. People who always wished they had

15 more minutes.

Some were the opposite – people whose demeaner suggested they had nothing to do. Their shoulders were loose, their bodies were loose, their jaws were loose, their eyes bored but wary. These folks were invariably supported by something – leaning against a wall, or standing with an elbow on a waste basket, as though they'd been so long without a watch telling them where to be and when to be there, they'd begun to fade, to melt, to meld into the walls and furnishings around them.

Most everyone, whether they were busying along or socially vestigial, fought the good fight against boredom by staring at their phones. Hardly anyone looked anyone else in the eye – ever! ("you're downtown CLEVELAND, for chrissake!") – and no one, no one at all, would dare look at a homeless person and risk having to engage. Have to acknowledge their humanity, have to be guilted into giving some "bum" your hard-earned money. Have to maybe listen to them, maybe even suffer their contagion, listen to their ramblings, their rantings.

A security guard in a booth had a momentary urge to get his weight off his chair and make a show of randomly rousting a homeless away from the station – he'd even tensed for an instant to get up – but the homeless man had presented a ticket, after all, and the guard's shift was almost over, so he went back to reading the Cleveland Plain Dealer Sports section and didn't budge.

The Other was otherwise as invisible as a panther in a closet as midnight. His zombie walk had included a thorough inspection of all the garbage cans of the underground station, filling his two black garbage bags like homeless Bluebeard digging up his treasure. He picked up a half-eaten piece of pizza off the ground, took a bite, and secreted away the rest into a pocket for later.

Once in the rail car, he put down his two bags, one on a chair and one beneath it, and stooped over to stare out the window intently. His MAGA hat with the brim extension obscured his face, but his tensed body suggested he was seeing something unusual, something odd, something important.

Outside the window there.

Without consciously deciding to, the other riders on the train peered out the window as well. While the others instinctively peered outside, the Other silently, liked a magician's misdirection, kicked the second bag on the ground further out of sight…. He then started coughing, picked up his other bag on the chair, and staggered off … to the brief relief of everyone else on board.

27

"Sargent Wharton! Sargent Wharton! This yours?" Jack Wharton was almost to his car when his journey home was interrupted by Ed Boretz, the gangly young marketing intern from Cleveland State University. Only a half hour before, a local paperboy, who was still inside the station Jack was now leaving, had positively identified

Ray Cardibello as their "person of interest". Now, there was work to do and his homemade crimelab was the best place to start.

"This hockey mask, it yours?" Ed was almost out of breath from running to catch the Sargent before he left.

"What?" Jack's brain wasn't really present to answer the question.

Intern Ed was slim – skinny almost – and eager. Very eager. He was brought in to help manage the department's Facebook page, but he was always looking for things to do, happy even to do "intern things" – made the coffee with a smile, asked if anyone needed anything filed, sometimes he even grabbed a broom. Good kid.

"This hockey mask. It yours?" Ed was holding a beat-up, old-style hockey mask — the kind former Cleveland Barons goaltender, Gerry Cheevers, used to wear when he was carving out a Hall of Fame career under the nickname, "Cheesy".

"I found it behind the lockers and it looked like it fell off the top of yours, maybe? Anyway, I understand you used to play, sir, and put two and two together, and thought you might want it?"

"Uh, oh yeah…emphasis on 'used to'…my old hockey mask…haven't seen that in years. How'd it ever get down here in the station? Behind a locker, you say? My locker?" Jack was confused.

"Sounds like a mystery, Sarge! No one better at solving mysteries than you!" Eager Ed grinned. "Probably a laundry sock gremlin," and Eager Ed grinned again.

"Yeah. Probably gremlins…" Jack's voice tailed off. "Well, who knows? No one ever cleans back there. Probably something I brought years ago and it just rose from the deep for no apparent reason, like Godzilla."

"Like who?" Ed was genuinely confused, but was eager to learn about who that was.

Jack chuckled. "Ask your father," and walked off absent-mindedly carrying a mask he couldn't remember the last time he wore.

28

The 4:44 pm Westbound Red Line was pulling out of the Tower City station, earlier than usual … at 4:55. The silver, light rail-cars slowly accelerated, looking like glistening aluminum baby ducks following their mother crossing a pond. Like most things exposed to the Cleveland elements, it was covered with a grime that seemed resistant by now to any cleaning agent or elbow grease. The windows were scratched as though every previous passenger who'd ever ridden in the car had run their nails along the glass panes on their way out.

Inside the car that an apparently-homeless man briefly wandered into, were the usual mixed commuter crowd. About half of the passengers were African-American. Most of the rest were White. The remaining few were random shades of yellow-ish, brown-ish, and tan-ish people color.

They carried themselves, for the most part, like every-one carries themselves when they're in their daily role as public transportation commuter. Different combinations of boredom, familiarity, and end-of-day relief blended together into a communal hypnosis – mesmerized into dullness from having lived the same familiar background sights and sounds over and over again. Going home by bus or rail, it's all the same buzz – people phase out and focus inward, mostly, while maintaining a background wariness, as not everyone who uses public transportation is well-intentioned. Or stable.

A loud gaggle of around five or six young African-American teens sat together in two rows of seats, one behind the other. The boys in the row in front kneeled and faced backward, over the backs of their seats, to chatter with the group seated behind them. The girls in the second row alternatively laughed, teased, texted, or pretended not to hear what the boys were saying, even though their voices were easily heard throughout the car.

Scattered randomly were downtown profession-als, mostly white, wearing Cleveland business winter uniforms – nice suits covered with a warm, long, high-quality coat. They appeared to have all passed by a mandatory-purchase kiosk which ensured they all were wearing the requisite scarf. These, mostly men, led lives too important to allow commuter minutes to pass by unproductively, and so peered into phones, laptops, or serious-looking reading material, although one older man wearing a dark blue raincoat on this sunny day was reading a newspaper.

Almost a third of the passengers were women, all of whom carried themselves with an invisible perimeter barrier– you could feel a social moat surrounded them and sense there would be consequences for trying to cross the upraised drawbridge. They encased themselves, through experience, in a private space exoskeleton.

Two young white couples, sitting in seats across the aisle, were obvious novice exceptions – their demeanor advertised their unfamiliarity with their surroundings, and they collectively seemed to be having a contest to see who could clench their shoulders and sphincters the tightest. Their suburban anxiety would scream "mug me" to anyone so inclined, but there were no criminals on this train.

Anymore.

The 4:44, which pulled out at 4:55, was actually due to arrive at the West Avenue – Cudell Station at 4:55. It's first stop, however, would be West Side Market. The 4:44 emerged from the underground Tower City station into the light of day, and began its journey across the bridge over the Cuyahoga River. Looking back, any passengers peering outward in the direction they'd just left, would see the downtown skyline, hard-pressed against the river shore. The grime and urban dinge that had coated the rail cars had been of the identical complexion that spread the same gray familial shade on every building. A rash of city gray over everything, like a snowfall of glum.

Looking back from the Cleveland Union Terminal Railway Bridge they were crossing, just south of the Veterans Memorial Bridge, were visible some of the city's 142 high-rises, including the tallest building in Cleveland – the 57-story Key Tower. Rising 947 feet on Public Square, looking like a non-descript, fat, Washington Monument with a red key on top, Key Tower had been the tallest building in Ohio since its completion in 1991.

Nearby, looking like Key Tower's once-mighty but now stooped and aged grandfather, stood the Terminal Tower, from whose Tower City bowels the Rapid Transit train had just emerged. The Terminal Tower showed its age, both nostalgically and quaintly. Born of the "skyscraper boom" of the 1920's and 1930's, the Tower looked like an old man that had once been "of means" – it's design hung over its frame like a high-quality suit that had gone out of style decades before. The Terminal Tower once stood as the tallest building in North America outside of New York city, until 1964. Now, were it really an old man with feelings, would have had to content itself humbly with being the second tallest building in Ohio.

The river below the bridge, the Cuyahoga, had been a "working river" – its history rich in use as an important form of transportation for Cleveland's industry. Of late, however, more trendy, upscale housing in the area had supported the development of the river as a recreational center, with bike paths and kayakers. On this day, the river was a shiny, meandering brown, like a wide streak of glistening, muddy toothpaste poured back and forth across the river valley.

As the train commuted along at a cozy 45 miles per hour, from the third car of five – the middle car – came a sound, a popping sound, like an M-80…or a low caliber gunshot.

It was November 11th, exactly 53 weeks after America had elected a new president. It was a perfectly clear, sunny, cold day in Cleveland.

29

Somewhere, Jack Wharton had a feeling. Something felt "wrong." Somehow, he felt like something very bad was going to happen. It made him feel anxious. It made him feel sad. It made him feel helpless…and what else… did it make him feel somehow … guilty? Could he… should he… be doing more?

30

The pipe-bomb in the bag the homeless-looking man had left behind in car number three wasn't particularly large and therefore not particularly noisy. Passengers who initially heard it at first thought it was perhaps a mechanical malfunction – a broken part in the undercarriage or maybe they'd just hit a rock.

The small, cylindrical explosive, however, wasn't alone in that bag. No, it was surrounded with and accompanied by a certain gelatinous substance – a gooey, gasoline-smelling, sticky substance that instantly was spread around the car's interior by the tiny pipe bomb…and then instantly burst into flame.

Passengers near the bag found themselves with the hot-burning napalm adhered to random body parts. This lady here had flames sprouting from her neck. That gentleman there – the one with the raincoat – was on fire from the back of his head and his left leg.

Those who were immediately splashed with the sticky flammable were shocked into instant panic from the agony of it. Some screamed and stared helplessly at their body parts as they disintegrated away forever right in front of their eyes. Others ran mindlessly, maddened by pain, taking off up and down the aisle, jumping over chairs, banging into other people, some of whom then became splashed themselves by the napalm, which then, like a rapidly spreading epidemic, enflamed the person newly infected … in a game of unintentional fire death tag.

Those not on fire, mirroring those who were, also responded in one of two ways. Some, terrified into frozen inaction, just sat there, as though they were patiently waiting to be tagged. Others sprang into actions – some of those actions, surprisingly, had a chance to be effective.

This latter group, of activists, ran to the ends of the car

and banged their bodies against the door like mating rams. Over and over they crashed themselves desperately into the doors, on each end, but the doors, designed to be locked when moving for safety, would not yield. Others tried to pry open the doors from which they'd entered, but these potential exits, too, refused to release those doomed inside.

A light came on in the driver's panel – the light no driver ever wants to see – the emergency fire light. Tyrone Jenkins had been driving for the RTS for 15 years. Had served in the Marines for four years before that. He was trained to respond effectively in an emergency. But, right now he was crossing the bridge over the Cuyahoga River 200 feet below. There was nowhere to stop. No place to go. He sped up his train to get to the next station as quickly as he could.

Inside the car, the shock had already worn off enough for those inside to really feel the pain of their bodies burning, and they screamed and writhed in agony. A couple of the business commuting men began to try to smash the glass to escape, banging shoes and laptops and suitcases against the windows that had already endured so many insulting, clouding scratches over the years.

Finally, one of the desperate blows against the glass succeeded, and the window cracked, shattered, and collapsed inward leaving the window space completely naked to the outside. But, a predictable calamity occurred at that point – the now fast-moving car, traveling over the lake, had generated substantial wind resistance and external air pressure.

The window, now exposed to the outside air pressure, acted similarly to how a window on a plane would act if broken at altitude, only in reverse. With a powerful whoosh, a huge gust of air, carrying with it a significant increase in oxygen, burst into the fiery chamber, which reacted as an old car engine would when a four-barrel carburetor kicks in – the flames that had been isolated, when fueled with the additional oxygen, grew explosively into one enormous fireball, blowing out the remaining windows and incinerating everything inside.

By the time Tyrone expertly raced his train to the West Side Market station and slammed the train to an emergency stop, the fire in car number three had already nearly burned itself out.

It would only be a few hours before someone spotted the graffiti painted on the Cleveland Union Terminal Railway Bridge, right below the exact spot where car number three caught fire…

…the graffiti on the bridge at that point said…

…. "The Other is the Other. That is All."

31

"Penny for your thoughts"

Jack Wharton had been staring out of his Berea home office for 15 straight minutes. He had been going over evidence with his long-time partner, the one he called

"Johnson", for hours and then he just… stopped and stared out the window.

It was cold in Cleveland. Now, with Thanksgiving only a few weeks away, the first snowfall had already lain a rough white veneer over the late autumn grey in a way that made everything seem both clean and new – baptized in renewal – while at the same time, making the landscape a colorless old movie or television show ….

Black stems, grey sky, white snow. Visually, it could have been a scene from I Love Lucy. Or Perry Mason. White bones, blackened skin…the landscape of a skeleton. Cold. Lifeless. Not even the cardinal that sometimes came by was around today to add a bloody dash of red.

Clank!

The sound of one of Johnson's empty Bud Lights bouncing off the basketball hoop above the waste basket brought Jack's attention away from the still-life morgue outside and back into their "Berea Batcave."

"I was just thinking." Jack made the most obvious statement of his life.

"No shit. You thinking how you gonna' catch this motherfucking Other? That is what we've been going over for days now, isn't it? No fingerprints. No one gets a good look at him. We THINK we see a homeless guy on film, but he may as well be a see-through phantom for all the good the crappy images we have of him." Johnson wasn't angry at Jack at all, but to an outside observer it would have sounded that way. "And, these fed' assholes acting like we stupid local cops all look like

Barney Fife. This is some shit we got going in Cleveland, now pard'ner. So, if you're thinking of THAT, join half the freaking planet!"

Jack briefly glanced outside again for only a moment and then looked down at his feet. He kept his gaze there the whole time he spoke as though he were conversing with his size 12 Red Wing Oxfords. Neither they, nor Johnson, interrupted.

"It's this whole Other thing that gets me," he began sharing his thoughts staring intently at his Red Wings audience, keeping intent eye contact with the eyelets. "My whole life, ever since I was a kid, I always wanted to belong, to be included, to be seen as part of the group. I wanted to be seen as belonging ... and just as good – the same – as anyone else. As everyone else."

Jack paused briefly, and raised his eyes now to make eye contact with his secondary audience, the cobweb above the overhead lamp. "There was a whole lot of hate growing up. A whole lot. A lot I don't remember – some psychology mumbo jumbo or other – but, I remember the feeling. I remember it like it was yesterday. People, even as children, hating, wanting to rend apart, tear to pieces, other people, other children, just because they were different, and I HATED that!! I HATED how they would look and talk and plan and plot, the things they'd say they'd do, the things they would do... I HATED the hate! I hated those who would see people who were different as not being one of them just because they were different."

He returned to face his shoes, which hadn't budged nor blinked, each eyelet staring wide open, impassively.

"And this guy. This nameless MONSTER! He WANTS to be seen as different! He even calls himself this bullshit 'Other'. Don't you see, Johnson?!? Don't you see?!?"

Johnson was as still and passive and unblinking as the Red Wings.

"It's not just that he IS slaughtering people! It's that he embraces the whole concept of being exactly what I've hated my entire life! The very notion of there being an 'other' – that any of us should ever be seen as 'other', as less than, as not one of us – is the poison I rejected my whole life!"

Now, Jack and Johnson both sat, each as still now as the two shoes he was wearing, the worn shoes that he'd taken so many hard life steps in.

"He's not just a random psycho to me, Johnson. He is my nightmare…."

"Well, then pard'ner," Johnson finally broke the monologue. "Then, let's make this nightmare go away. Let's go over what we have … again."

And, they began to go down the trail of dust that they tried to pretend had leads…again.

"Question one. Do we still think it could be this Cardibello fellow? Question two. If so, why hasn't he turned up? Question three…"

And, as Johnson went over the key issues of the case,

point by point, as methodically as a blind ant searching a kitchen cupboard for a crumb in the corner – AGAIN – Jack glanced briefly at the front page headline emblazoned above the fold of the Cleveland Plain Dealer.

TERROR STRIKES CLEVELAND / NATIONAL MANHUNT FOR "PERSON OF INTEREST"

Who is the Other?

32

"See that! Right there! There he goes again! He's Houdini!" The agent from the Federal Bureau of Investigations was amazed and frustrated. He'd been staring at video footage without sleep for days. "Look, how he dips his head right at the angle that his face would otherwise come into view. Here! Look! Just as he rounds the corner, he raises his bag to block the camera mounted on the Northwest, looking like he's taking a drink from whatever's inside it. Exactly 32 seconds later, as he should have been visible from the Eastbound driver's camera, he stumbles behind a post. I've never seen anything like it! *Verschlungen* Houdini!"

Agent Sjoltsen Vinjrud had watched every video recovered from every camera for 10 square city blocks. He had watched video footage from storefronts cameras, cell phones, security cameras, news cameras – video from every square foot of the area was being forwarded to investigators. Every moment of our lives in 2018 is permanently recorded – the trails that each and every one of us follow are recorded. There is no place in the urban landscape that anyone can go and not be caught on some type of camera.

Always.

The Boston Marathon bombers were eventually identified through this type of investigation – they were traced backward from the moment the bomb exploded – a snippet from this storefront camera showing them leaving behind the backpack, a few moments from this cell phone showing them walking down the street – each video a time machine tracking the killers back, step by step, until eventually, the trail led to exactly where they were. Random pictures from random cameras from random people piece together a puzzle of pedestrians – a parade of the mundane – each of us Hansel and Gretel leaving digital bread crumbs that don't lead us home, but can lead an investigator to where our homes are.

So, why wasn't it working now? Agent Vinjrud had to know.

"I just don't get it." He explained the video evidence anomaly of this case to the 12-person lead investigative team pursuing the terrorist who had left behind a bomb on an RTA light rail train. These dozen lead investigators, in turn, directed an army of agents and officers compiled from every law enforcement agency in the federal government, the state of Ohio, and of course, the City of Cleveland. Representing the city detectives, and therefore low man on the totem pole sitting in the back,

Jack Wharton was trying to understand it all himself.

"It's hard to imagine what type of person would even know all those cameras were even there, let alone their exact location. Even crazier still is to shuffle about like some drunk guy while keeping his face from being cleanly photographed. He's either the luckiest guy on the planet… or…"

"What if it's just that? You know, sometimes they say that a drunk guy will survive a car crash that would have killed someone sober. Maybe, it's really just dumb luck and he just keeps staggering around like that because he is drunk and our cameras just happen to be in the wrong place?" Chief Patrolman Buddy O' Malley was a good cop. Representing the Ohio State Highway Patrol, he was asking the question that needed to be asked… so it could be eliminated. That wasn't why he asked it, but it was an honest question from an honest officer trained to be a leader in the Highway Patrol…not a lead investigator of terrorism.

"I'm sorry, what's your name?" it was important to Agent Vinrud that he be professional and polite. He was accustomed to patiently providing expert answers to questions posed by non-experts.

"Buddy. Buddy O' Malley from the State Highway Patrol"

"Thank you, Officer…err, Buddy" Vinrud almost fell into the Norwegian accent of his upbringing and just avoided stretching out the "u" sound in a way that would make it sound like three syllables, all sounding like the "u" in "glue".

"Maybe 20, 30 years ago that might have been true," the FBI's leading authority on media forensics and video evidence began. "Back then, people would just put security cameras randomly throughout a space environment in places where they thought made sense. The angle, height, focus field, quality of video, cameral composition footprint, strategic directional cross-mapping – all of the matrix coverage points and anticipated pathway tendencies – they were just randomly chosen. In those days, the video evidence of a crime, IF it were even successfully recorded, was just as likely to be of someone's feet or pants as their face."

Patrolman O' Malley was already regretting asking the question.

"Today, the placement of cameras in a high-traffic public security space like Tower City, quite literally, isn't an art. It's a science. It's called Video Surveillance Psychometry, or VSP for short. Ever since 9/11, a concerted effort has been placed on applying scientific analysis, game theory, and big data to the design of passive detection design. Before money is wasted on any equipment, a statistical analysis is made of pedestrian traffic – not anticipated traffic, but the footflow in actuality. Data. Acquired through research.

"Do most people turn left or right when they walk around the support post? What percentage of way traffic stop and get a drink from this fountain? How many people look up at this sign? What height range do 95%

of passersby fall? When do most people begin to turn left around this corner, and where are they typically facing when they do? All of these factors are then converted into a three-dimensional probability matrix which then guides the placement of the cameras.

 "Overlain on top of all of that is the stealth planning of the camera design. How to make the cameras themselves as unobtrusive as possible, to make them blend into the design environment in a way that makes them most unlikely to be spotted", Vinrud knew he was sounding professorial but it was imperative the investigation team understood the significance of his findings.

"The odds of someone randomly turning and twisting, blocking each and every camera's view by sheer chance are astronomical. No, somehow, not only did this murderer know the location of every camera location and angle throughout the view matrix field, but he had to have pre-planned each move throughout the commuter space."

Vinrud's voice still sounded flat, so when he paused for effect, there was no effect.

"Don't you get it?" Vinrud finally raised his voice. "Very few people even KNOW where those cameras are! This psycho not only knew where they were – ALL of them – but he planned – PLANNED! – like some macabre dance, a series of innocuous-looking moves that would allow him to walk through this heavily secure viewspace, unseen… like a ghost.…"

"So, he's a security expert then? Maybe a contractor or

consultant?" O' Malley was determined to say something that made up for his previous question.

"That's one angle we're working. But, there's another thing. Another highly anomalous event, like two bullets striking each other in mid-air. There is no video of this homeless-looking 'Other' entering the building, or leaving it.

"He seemed to come out of nowhere. He's first seen at point X on gate entrance camera 4B. Right here. Here he stumbles to the gate, inserts his ticket, and stumbles through. There is no video of his having bought a ticket, although he could have bought it at any station.

"He's last seen at point Z, on exit camera 7C. There is the last image. Off he stumbles with his one remaining bag up this hallway into a video blind spot… and then, he's just gone. Nothing, not a hint, of him anywhere in the area for blocks around. We're looking at video for hours before and after. Nothing."

"He had to come from somewhere. He's not a goddamn ghost! He's motherfucking flesh and blood. He HAS to be there!" Cleveland's Chief of Police Calvin D. Williams was a no-nonsense man. He'd grown up on the streets of Cleveland. He didn't believe in ghosts, and he wasn't afraid of any man. He also had to drive past the Cleveland Union Terminal Railway Bridge every single day on his way to work in the early morning, and then back again late in the evening…on those nights when he even went home.

Vinrud just stared with his jaw open.

"I don't give a flying fuck for your goddamn matrix! This isn't a Keanu Reeves movie! This is real life. That motherfucker walked into that Tower City station. He walked out. A camera somewhere HAD to catch a picture of him. It HAD to!"

Vinrud slowly walked back to the laptop. He had more raw footage to show the team – raw footage of angle after angle not showing any homeless man.

Jack Wharton was sitting in the back trying like everyone else to make sense of what he was hearing. By coincidence, he'd just re-read Edgar Allen Poe's The Purloined Letter on a recent night, one of many, when sleep wouldn't come easy, if at all.

"Maybe, he's hidden in plain sight?" Jack asked.

Vinrud walked over to the digital dry erase brainstorm board, the one that had been covered, recorded, erased over and over again since the Investigation team first assembled. "Hidden in plain sight", he wrote in large red letters. And circled it before going back to his laptop.

33

"Could your Cardibello DO all that?" Johnson was incredulous after Wharton brought him up to speed on the investigation. "This all sounds like a man with training. Maybe, CIA or KGB. He strangled that badass Altuve without getting a scratch. Now, he can walk around invisible to cameras and disappear like some

Ninja? Who is he – Kwai Chang Caine? You're telling me some jackass loser from your neighborhood can do all that? What kind of neighborhood did you grow up in?"

Jack had just enjoyed this exact same conversation with the 12-person lead investigative team, who had asked the exact same question. And, he gave the exact same answer. "Even though he's psychopathic enough to commit these atrocities, I think it's unlikely that Ray Cardibello could do what this 'Other' has done. However, I think it's highly unlikely that ANYONE could have done what this 'Other' has done!

"There is no mass murderer school that trains people to do this! People blather on about Al Qaeda training camps and how brilliant the 9/11 attacks were. That's bull. All they did was take some basic flight lessons, buy some plane tickets, and pack boxcutters.

"There is no training ground for this. So, in answer to your question – Cardibello is the only lead we've got. We know he was at the scene of the first crime. He's our target. He's the man we're going to get."

Now, it was Johnson's turn to look out the window. He looked at his partner, eye to eye.

"And, if it ain't him...?"

They held their gaze two more beats. Then, Johnson sat back down on the table below the Lebron James poster, pulled out the folder marked "last known acquaintances" for the fifth time that day, and started clicking on his laptop. The two working alone together in their

Berea Bat Cave. And, Johnson never even finished his half-open Bud Light.

34

The Cleveland Greyhound bus station, located on East 14th and Chester, is a lonely place at night. The art deco structure, built in 1948, is like much of the city. Once a sparkling landmark, now drab with layers of smog – tarnished and worn by time, tight budgets, and harsh exposure to Cleveland winters.

It nonetheless maintains an iconic reputation among historical architects – it's swooping curved lines resemble a ship at sea, as though it is floating atop soaring waves instead of being surrounded by concrete in the middle of a downtown parking lot ocean. It's tall vertical sign stands as a mast hoisting the GREYHOUND banner – a modern day Jolly Roger. Instead of skull and cross-bones, the mast had the distinctive company logo of the running dog, flying in mid-stride. The clock atop the mast was rarely right, nowadays, more than twice a day.

Again, like much of Cleveland, the building is a worn holdover of a noble past in the middle of a present-tense, surprisingly bustling urban setting, called Playhouse Square. The nearby Hofbrauhaus, to the southeast, is the latest new social magnet attracting local hipsters, hopesters, downtown residents, and suburban young adults out to catch the new "downtown vibe."

The station is big, with 20 gates, 28 in-bound and 29 outbound routes a day – in fact, too big. Despite the Cleveland stop being among the busiest in the entire national chain, Greyhound has plans to move its location. A new use for the historic, old transportation hub is being discussed sparking a debate – like everything else in Cleveland – between those who argue for preserving the past traditions and those who are eager to outgrow Cleveland's being seen as "backward" by other communities.

If some concerned traveler were to Google the station, they would come across passengers asking whether the station is a safe place to wait for a bus in the wee hours. This is another holdover from a time when 14th and Chester invoked a sense of urban decay and inner-city poverty – a place where "white boys" from the suburbs wouldn't think about going at night. The area was never as violent as its reputation, but the young students from nearby Cleveland State University were generally advised to avoid the area after dark. And, they usually did. Back in the day.

Today, for people who live in the city, as opposed to wary cross-country bus travelers, the area is known more for the bustling Cleveland Playhouse. Founded in 1915 and recipient of the 2015 Regional Theatre Tony Award, their website proclaims the Playhouse as being "America's first professional regional theatre." Among its historical quirks, the Playhouse is where Margaret Hamilton, the Wicked Witch of Oz, made her stage debut in 1927. The Greyhound station is one block of parking lot desert north of the Cleveland Playhouse.

On this day, waiting in a corner booth behind a day-old Cleveland Plain Dealer, a certain Cleveland native was planning to be one of the bus line's 19.3 million annual passengers.

This man was olive-skinned, with lusty, flowing black hair like Victor Mature. His build was a squat six feet and muscular, like a block – yet he moved lightly on his feet, planting a footfall that never made a sound. He had high cheekbones and a fine complexion, for a middle-aged man who'd spent too many nights outdoors. Once considered handsome, he was as worn from the elements as the Greyhound building he was now sitting in.

His clothing could best be described as "urban invisible." Dark grey pants, sensible, Black, winter shoes, Cleveland Browns hooded sweatshirt – he looked as non-descript as any of the garbage cans placed throughout the building. Looking identically alike – each an unrecognizable twin to the others.

Only if someone could see his eyes would he stand out – would his unique other-ness become visible. Only if someone could see those eyes would he stand out and become any more visible than the invisible posters on the wall telling people to surrender their seats for seniors, pregnant women, and people with disabilities.

Those eyes.

Twin black holes whose gravitational force was too powerful to allow any kind thought, caring gesture, or the slightest empathy or concern for another human being to escape. Eyes that had witnessed pain, had witnessed violence, had witnessed others pleading for mercy, had seen so many wrongs on others' bodies and spirits performed — seen them performed as final acts would be performed at the nearby Playhouse… but his shows would have no Deus Ex Machina miraculous happy endings. No, the shows of real-world violence witnessed by these burning eyes, committed by the hands connected to them, never had a happy ending.

For anyone.

Eyes that had seen nothing but unhappy endings. Hands that had done nothing but physically write those conclusions onto other people's life stories. A two-legged playwright of pain, those eyes were the director.

There was one other feature the man had that would have stood out, if anyone was unlucky enough to see it. It was a distinctive reddish/pink line, a line that zigzagged back and forth randomly, like a clumsy drunk painter ruined someone's portrait with one brush stroke. This meandering line, which extended from the right corner of his mouth almost to his ear, was even more rarely seen than the man's eyes.

Over the years, the man had developed a knack − a knack of moving his face in ways that never let that side of his face be seen. Not fully. And, anyone who looked at him at all − if they would actually see past his urban chameleon camouflage to catch a glimpse of his face, would first see those poisoned eyes − and would immediately look away. They wouldn't know why, but an instinct would tell them to look away… and miss seeing the scar. And, their instincts were right.

Otherwise, he was invisible.

It didn't matter that the man's face was on the news and in all the papers. All that mattered, in the streets of Cleveland, is that some men's faces you knew better than to look at.

It was 3 am.

And, the man was thinking of catching a bus.

He thought this was a good time.

But, not today. Tomorrow would be better.

Tomorrow would be just fine.

35

The 12-person investigative team, as professionals inured to the horrors of atrocities will do, enjoyed the camaraderie of gallows humor. They called themselves Team "Just Another" – a play on the name the man they were pursuing had given himself. If he thought of himself as "The Other", then to them, he'd be considered "Just Another". It was Highway Patrol Officer Buddy O' Malley's idea of Irish wit – he was determined to say something the others would think wasn't just something a "simple Mick" might say. The name stuck. Team "Just Another" it was.

Eventually, the name was abbreviated to Team JA, which soon acquired the pronunciation of the German word for "yes" (Vinrud's idea). Thus was born the "JA Team", pronounced "Ya Team."

One day some anonymous person on the team went a step too far with their creative branding, at least in the opinion of one very intense man. Atop the dry erase board they used for initial concept brainstorming, someone had taped a paper that said "*Ja, wir koennen*", or German for "Yes, we can" playing off the "JA" acronym for their team.

That was not a great idea in the opinion of Cleveland's Chief of Police Calvin D. Williams. No, Chief Williams was not amused. The wiry Chief, who had kicked down more doors in the city than maybe anyone else in Cleveland's history, was not amused at all.

When he saw the sign, he slowly walked over to it. He looked at it like someone had vomited on the altar at his beloved Antioch Baptist Church — Cleveland's second-oldest African-American Baptist Church where "You'll find Jesus from the moment you park your car in our secured parking lot."

The room, which had been buzzing with pre-meeting energy, dimmed to silence when the Chief slowly pulled the sign from the board gently, without breaking the tape that was used to adhere it. He stared at it again when it was in his hand, as though he were deep in thought, and then slowly, slowly, looked up and deeply into each pair of eyes that were now watching him.

As he looked each team member in the eye, he would tear the paper in his hand very, very slowly, and each person he was looking at would cringe like it was part of their own bodies being torn apart in a mirror in front of them.

One by one, the Chief silently looked at the other 11 and made one tear on the sheet. He then carefully placed the torn pieces on the table in the center of the room where they stayed for three days in an untouched pile that no one ever mentioned – until one morning … they just weren't there anymore.

Nearly all the members of the 12-member JA team had served in the military. Most of them had seen action. But, none of them had any desire to get on the wrong side of Cleveland's Chief of Police.

"So, we're working on a new theory." FBI Agent Sjoltsen Vinjrud was back with another presentation analyzing the video evidence. "We're investigating the hypothesis that the terrorist in question somehow changed his clothes into a different disguise when he was in one of the camera system's blind spots."

The "terrorist in question" was the term that the team had come to use in describing their prey, as they didn't want to give him the satisfaction of being called "The Other", even behind closed doors. And, of course, when Agent Sjoltsen said "question", it came out sounding like "kvestion", one of the rare occasions his Nordic background became apparent.

"Good! Good!" The Chief liked where this was going.

"Well, good and not so good." Agent Vinjrud was exact, detail-oriented, and methodical. Until he had a final solution that was definitive, everything to that point was all still "undetermined and speculative".

The Chief grimaced. Friends of his had people on that doomed Rapid Transit car.

"While we see potential in this line of inquiry, the hypothesis has a hole." The room could feel the air about to be taken out of the hopeful theory offered only seconds before.

"We have looked at the video of every man, woman and child who walked into that hallway where the terrorist in question was last seen. If this hypothesis is correct, one additional person, the terrorist in disguise, should have walked out of that tunnel. Someone should have been filmed coming out of the tunnel but not coming in. If we could find that person, we'd likely have our terrorist.

"But, we don't see anyone come out who did not come in."

"What does that mean?" Patrolman O' Malley was confused like everyone else.

The Chief's voice was next. "It means we keep looking."

The meeting moved onto the next item on the agenda – surveillance of known hangouts for Cleveland's homeless population. But Jack Wharton, who had sat silently in the back as he usually did, glanced over at the circled words written now on an easel sheet marked "retained brainstorm inquiries." Those words, "hidden in plain sight" taunted his brain now more than ever. "There's something there" he thought to himself. "Something we're just not seeing."

36

Jack was panicking. He was laying atop a field of clovers, searching desperately for the one with four leaves. Only they all had four leaves … until he picked one up. Then, when he looked at what had been a four-leaf clover, he instead saw what looked like a reflection in his hand – only "his" reflection had a scar.

He kept frantically scanning the vast field he was laying atop – his hands grasping, clawing, stroking, scratching like his fingers were kneading bread or striking the keys on a massive green piano. He kept seeing nothing but 4-leaf clovers – and that's what he was looking for, wasn't it? – but each time, each time over and over, when he picked up the clover, the same transformation would occur – he'd be holding his own reflection, or what resembled his own reflection but wasn't… with a scar.

He got up off the ground and began running, every-where he looked was green, up, down, left, right – the sky was filled with 4-leaf clovers now mocking him, laughing as he ran, the green panorama swirling around him as he spun in circles – like a Merry-Go-Round in a green fishbowl.

He suddenly thought he was Eli Wallach running around

the graveyard in the movie "The Good, The Bad, and the Ugly," which he watched as a kid. Looking for a grave marker now, the one that marked the gold, the one with the name "Arch Stanton" on it.

Only he wasn't "Tuco" from the movie. He was himself as a little boy, running to keep away from all the Italian boys in the neighborhood. And, they were laughing too, but he kept running only now he was running in slow motion and he wanted to get away so badly he found the grave marked "Arch Stanton" and he began to dig – to dig underground, and under the gravestone of the grave marked "Arch Stanton" wasn't a coffin but a large grey room, a room with an exit sign.

Jack could feel that this was his way out, the way out he desperately needed, only he could barely move, could barely move on his hands and knees, could barely move on his hands and knees in the large grey room toward the sign marked "exit", it took his supreme effort to crawl, to crawl forward toward that sign, the sign marked exit, only now the sign was pulling away, pulling away in smoke, he had to catch it, had to catch it – NOW! TODAY! HE HAD TO CATCH IT!

He could hear the boys outside – the scary ones he'd grown up with, start to come down into the large grey hall too. He heard a voice "Tickets please? Tickets?"

Was that his mother's voice?!?

Jack Wharton woke up.

He took a pull, no, 2 pulls, off the bottle of Fireball he kept at his bedside for just such occasions. Long ones.

He dried himself off using the bedside towel he kept for the same reason. He looked at the clock.

Four am.

He turned on the light. It was two weeks before Christmas and he could see his neighbor's bloated white inflatable yard-Santa glowing outside.

He took another pull.

Jack walked into the bathroom and splashed cold water on his face. Somewhere a light had come on – Jack somehow felt he knew something he had no business knowing.

He had a hunch.

And work to do if he were going to get ready.

37

Rust belt cities are tough. They have to be. The winters are rough, the summers are rough, the economy is rough, their upbringings are rough. Cleveland is no exception. Its roots are rough-hewn which has imbued within the community's culture a strong work ethic and community spirit. People pull together to survive the winters and hard work is respected.

Like everywhere, Cleveland's culture today was founded by the generations who came before. Most of the migration to Cleveland occurred between 1870 and 1914. People from "the old country" with strong backs and a willingness to work hard were needed in Cleveland's steel mills, petroleum refineries, coach factories, lumberyards, and canal boats.

They were Poles, Irish, Czechs, Slovaks, Germans, English, Scots, Slovenians, Serbians, Croatians, Hungarians, Bulgarians, Romanians, Russians, Lithuanians, Greeks, Hispanics, Ukrainians and people from two dozen other nations.

Like today, migration to America at the time was often driven by shortages, hardships, and persecutions in their home countries. They thought they were coming to a land of gold-paved streets, but they usually spent their lives working twelve hours a day, six days a week, for low wages, often in unsafe workplaces.

The breakout of the first World War made immigration from abroad more difficult. At the same time, wartime industries in places like Cleveland had an increased demand for labor. This demand was largely met by African Americans relocating from the American South.

Cleveland has had African-American families living there from its earliest history, but it had a relatively small Black population of around 10,000 immediately before the war. By 1920, the figure had grown to 34,451, and 20 years later, stood at over 85,000. It was also in the 1920s that Cleveland received its first significant group of Spanish-speaking immigrants from Mexico.

In many ways, Cleveland represents the melting pot American ideal of success being a result of hard work, taking risks, and supporting each other to get ahead.

Clevelanders help their neighbors, and they expect people who can work, to work. Many Clevelanders have deep, committed roots in mostly-Christian or Jewish faiths that mandate aid for the poor and non-judgmentalism towards those who have less. Yet, there are still many who struggle to respect any homeless person who is physically sound enough to get a job and doesn't.

This bi-polar relationship with the homeless was exacerbated after the terror brought upon the city by the Other. While Clevelanders' commitment to helping the poor and the homeless – particularly through the harsh winter – was unwavering, there was still a renewed sense building throughout the community that the homeless were "the problem."

Attacks against the homeless, verbal and physical, rose. Contributions to charities helping the homeless shrunk. Empathy toward the homeless waned. Fear of the homeless grew.

Visually, this could be seen by the enormous police presence in every setting where homeless were known to congregate, live, and receive services. At the City Mission at 53rd and Carnagie, rotating triads of Black-uniformed military-looking figures walked around carrying Uzi's hugged to their chests – 24 hours a day, seven days a week. A similar team patrolled the Lutheran Memorial Ministry's Men's Shelter at 2100 Lakeside, the largest shelter in the state of Ohio.

Everywhere the homeless were known to be, teams of officers, investigators, and military anti-terrorism teams were highly visible – questioning, documenting, finger-printing, tracking – it was as though open hunting season were declared on Cleveland's homeless, only fortunately, the hunt was "catch and release"… for now.

Lead investigators, from the beginning, doubted that this "Other" was a random homeless person who would be caught from such a broad dragnet, but this local effort was coordinated by Cleveland's Police Chief, and even if all he were doing was eliminating the possibility their suspect was amongst the homeless population, he was damn sure going to do it right.

The city was changing, morphing, evolving to accommodate this new threat, like a species of animal adapting to an epidemic of some new, foreign disease. Companies like Uber and Lyft began marketing escort walking services – a new part of the gig economy where the services of having someone walk alongside you was part of a new app.

A robust volunteer pedestrian escort network also emerged, "The Believeland Valet Walkers", to "walk anywhere, anytime, for any reason" alongside their fellow Clevelander. Gun sales rose, gun training classes had waiting lists, memberships in self-defense training boomed. Cameras were installed. Private security was everywhere.

All types of locals – hipsters, construction workers, college instructors on break – were offended, angered, or amused at being taken for homeless and questioned. Sales of "I'm not homeless" buttons were brisk.

Yet, the Other remained unfound.

And tonight, on this night, one man with a sought-after face was going to try to find a way through and out of this law-enforcement Pac Man maze.

He was going to buy a ticket to take a bus.

Neil Kendricks-Johnson was making a guest presentation to the lead investigation team, which was now always called Team "Just Another." After the Chief of Police expressed his displeasure, the team abandoned all the catchy-sounding nicknames they had been acquiring as a result of their global profile. Now, they were always "Team Just Another", a reminder of the disdain they expressed for their prey, who called himself "the Other."

Kendricks-Johnson was invited in to elaborate on the psychological profile they had created by the lead profile experts the Feds brought in. Officially, Kendricks-Johnson was brought in to provide a "local perspective", but the reality was the profile they had been building was leading them nowhere and the team finally surrendered to the requests of the Chief to bring in their local forensics expert. And, Kendricks-Johnson, known as "the Professor", was considered a genius by the local police.

As often happened to the Professor, when he first came in, he was mistaken for the janitor. A dark bear of a man, with a lumbering gait, broad nose and Jeri-curl isn't the image typically conjured when one thinks of a "Professor". When Kendricks-Johnson walked in, one of the Feds got shirty.

"Excuse me, sir. Sir? This is a restricted area. You'll have to come back later to empty the wastebaskets. If we need them emptied sooner, we'll put in a request, but for now, we'll have to ask you to continue on your rounds."

FBI Agent Thomas Gibson had graduated top of his class from Alabama's Regis University Master of Science in Criminology program. He had impressed the group with his diligence in reading reports and was an encyclopedia of knowledge about terrorist attacks around the globe. He had worked hard to rid himself of his childhood southern drawl as he'd long-since understood his "twang" might mean "uneducated hillbilly" to those outside of Alabama.

Up until now, he also had one saving grace on the team. He didn't talk too much.

"Sir? Sir! Do I need to call your supervisor and report that you are disobeying the lawful order of an official agent of the Federal Bureau of Investigation?" and Gibson let a bit of his Southern accent contort the pronunciation of "Bureau" to sound more like "Bur E Oh". The Professor continued ambling his large frame toward the computer in the front of the room, oblivious to the "lawful order" of the Fed.

Just when it appeared Gibson was considering whether to draw his gun, in walked Cleveland Police Chief Calvin D. Williams.

Immediately recognizing what was happening, the Chief simply said "I see you've met the Professor." He said it blankly, as matter-of-factly as someone mentioning it was starting to drizzle outside.

Gibson turned as red as the uniforms on his beloved Crimson Tide football team. No other mention was made over the confusion. It was just another everyday occurrence people of color lived with in Cleveland, Ohio.

"I understand that you've already been briefed on the 'typical' origin dynamics of these type of serial killers" Kendricks-Johnson began his presentation right on time, as the last few straggling members of the team scurried to their chairs. Despite the Professor's imposing physique, his voice was thin and reedy. If you closed your eyes, you could imagine that voice coming out of a scrawny academic figure leading a lecture in a college classroom. Only if you opened your eyes would the illusion disappear as his voice seemed a cartoonish mismatch to his massive frame, like something substituted by a nearby ventriloquist.

"I see that you've delved into the cliché, yet valid, descriptions of how these monster men are created. A childhood of abuse and victimization resulting in deep-seated psychological trauma. This trauma, in turn, becomes buried, denied, stuffed into a closet from whence it grows more and more powerful.

"As time goes on, a variety of coping mechanisms are created to allow the individual to appear to function normally. Amnesia over traumatizing experiences, the development of imaginary friends, the disconnecting of feelings, the inability to bond with another human being, substance abuse – all these, as your profile to this point describe, are the current understanding of how the seeds of eventual destruction are planted.

"Over time, these coping mechanisms start breaking down. They stop working. The demons inside, having been stuffed tighter and tighter, become stronger, like compressing a spring. Eventually, the spring needs to be released, and they lash out in ways that, ironically, mirror the traumas that were once inflicted upon them."

The team listened politely. They'd heard this all before and it just made for so much background elevator music at this point. Gibson was the only one intently taking notes, as he couldn't bear to make eye contact with the African-American genius he'd mistaken for the janitor.

"What I haven't seen in your reports however" the Professor continued, "is the answer to the question 'why now?' Has anyone thought to ask why this 'Other' didn't start killing people a month ago, or a year ago, or five years from now?"

"But, Professor, why do crazy people ever do anything?" Highway Patrolman Buddy O' Malley was the one member of the team who would ask the question everyone else didn't want to ask because it would make them look stupid. "I mean, crazy is crazy, isn't it? By definition, that means there is no reason for when or why, or am I just being me old daft self agin'?"

"That's such a great question, Patrolman O' Malley." The Professor liked the Irish Patrol Officer. "It's essential, as we construct our model, to never forget that models aren't people. Even the best model is full of suppositions, built upon assumptions, and held together by guesses.

"It's exactly this dynamic that led me to identify the critical oversight in the original model to this point. Every fault line eventually fails and breaks, causing an earthquake at an unpredictable point in time. So, when we build a psychological model, we assume the same applies to people. There is a random starting point to the behaviors – that's just the point in time that this man happened to break. Because, as you say, he's crazy.

"But, we're overlooking the obvious" the Professor's voice somehow became darker, more abdominal, like he'd taken some of the restraining governor's off of it that he used to keep from scaring people.

 "Don't you see? It's like some of the models for cancer. The thinking with cancer is that there is a genetic disposition, which lies dormant until something sets if off. So, an individual goes their entire life with a latent disposition for getting lung cancer which lies dormant... until they start smoking. That smoking event then activates the gene to cause cancer."

The team stared. Even Gibson.

"This isn't just a random psycho. He's a crusader" the Professor's voice briefly boomed, before resuming its usual thin presence. "He's killing for a cause. To his mind

– to HIS warped mind – there is a REASON behind all this. A rationale. Some greater good that justifies his killings."

The team tracked the Professor's thinking but couldn't see where it was going. People could rarely see where the local forensics genius was going, until he led them there.

"So, for THIS killer, there had to be some 'thing' – some EVENT – that triggered him. For him, this isn't a random seeking of relief. This is a purposeful series of behaviors intent on creating an outcome. If we can identify the triggering event, we might get a clue as to who he might be."

"I thought this Other is this here Cardibello feller."

The Professor was less kind to O' Malley's comment this time.

"And, if he isn't…?"

The team sat in silence for a full five seconds. The thought of their chief, and only suspect, not being the killer was daunting enough. The thought of their chief suspect being innocent, AND not having any other suspects or leads made them swallow hard and their sphincters tighten. People were dying and the world was watching.

"So, where now, Professor" the Chief of Police wasn't one to hesitate when action is called for.

"Now, Chief, we brainstorm recent local events in Cleveland that may have triggered this 'Other' to start killing people." This was where the Professor had intended to lead the team from the start.

"So, what has happened in Cleveland recently that might trigger someone?" O' Malley asked and some of the local team members held back snickers. Even the crusty Chief of Police had to wipe off a grin with that.

"Well, the Huffington Post declared Cleveland the Worst City in the World" came a voice from the back.

"What the fuck? That's going to trigger a serial murderer!" the voice of another Fed, the only female on the team, was feeling fed up.

"We're brainstorming," the Professor explained. "At this stage, we write down EVERYTHING. Otherwise, we self-edit and might miss out on the key idea," and the large Black man in front wrote down on the easel "Huff Post – C is World's Worst City."

"Gentlemen, the floor is open," the Professor prompted.

"Well, we had the Republican National Convention"

"So, we're looking for someone with an 'I'm with Her' bumper sticker?" O' Malley asked, sounding serious.

The Professor laughed and wrote down "look for 'I'm with Her' bumper stickers". That completely changed the mood. Now, the dam broke.

"The Browns lost all their games!"

"Schools suck!"

"Ariel Castro held three women captive for 10 years", Gibson was still embarrassed, but he was on the team for a reason "Serial killer Michael Madison was convicted in May 2016 for the murders of three East Cleveland women. In 2009, Cleveland Police discovered 11 dead women in Anthony Sowell's East Cleveland home."

And, the list of potential triggers grew into a pile of bread crumbs the team hoped to use, like Hansel and Gretel, to find their way home to one they were looking for.

39

"You know, Jack, there are times I almost wish I could join you at one of your YA Team meetings. They sound better than Gilligan's Island reruns on ME TV. You've even got the Professor. All you're missing is Ginger and Mary Anne!" Johnson was more amused than Jack expected in hearing what the team had been doing.

"Tell you what, Johnson. I'd love to see that Professor on Jeopardy. That big dude is SMART!" Jack, like everyone else on the team, was blown away by Neil Kendricks-Johnson, who had that rare intellect people could feel.

"Better yet, Jack, I'd love to BET on him on Jeopardy! Who'd ever guess a giant Black guy like that was a freaking genius?!"

Jack let that pass without comment, as he usually did with his long-time partner's inappropriate comments.

"Oh, and never let anyone hear you call it anything other than Team Just Another, whatever you do!"

"You'll never hear me call it anything other than the official name… outside the Batcave."

Above the fireplace, the Cavs game was playing on the Berea Batcave official game set with the sound off. Neither man knew the score.

"Look outside, Johnson. See anything?"

"Another crappy December day in Cleveland… oh look! There's a guy carrying an 'I am the Other' sign!"

"No, I mean look over there. I've been seeing this all around town. Mr. Wilson is walking with the kids to school. He's volunteered for Mondays. Ex-Marine. Mrs. Vansegheterat has Tuesdays. She was in my advanced handgun class. Carries two weapons. She can use 'em too.

Johnson watched Mr. Wilson walking with the children, his head subtly on a swivel.

"People are coming together. Pulling together against a common enemy. It's sick that it's taken this, but I've never seen the city like this. I've talked to neighbors I never even knew lived here. Each one coming up to me, not asking for help, but asking how they can help out".

"I'll drink to that, pard'ner" and Johnson handed Jack a Johnny Walker Red Label on the rocks.

Jack took the drink, tapped glasses, and took a nice gulp.

"You know, Johnson, the Professor is a genius and all,

but I still think it's going to come down to one thing. A hunch."

"You think you got one, Jack?"

"We'll see, pard'ner. We'll see."

40

Since at least the late 19th Century, authors have used the term "urban jungle" to describe inner-city life. In 1887, Arthur Conan Doyle's Dr. Watson described London as "that great cesspool into which all loungers and idlers of the Empire are irresistibly drained". T. S. Eliot, General William Booth of the Salvation Army, and Jack London have all compared people living in urban areas to animals living in wild, untamed jungles.

In 1920s Chicago, American sociologist Nels Anderson studied "hobos", urban culture, and work culture. He, too, used the metaphor of "jungle" to describe life in the urban environment.

Survival of the fittest.

Predators and prey.

A jungle.

In the city.

An Urban Jungle.

A primordial cesspool where one's struggles for life may need come at the expense of another's loss of life. Where loungers and idlers are irresistibly drained.

Travelers waiting at 3 am to catch a bus in Cleveland's downtown Greyhound station are unlikely to have read any of Dr. Anderson's sociology papers from the 1920s. Neither are they likely to be reading, while they wait, T.S. Eliot or Jack London. But, they will understand in their gut their role as creatures in that jungle

Cleveland's urban jungle.

Those either sober or awake would probably be staring at their phones, hacking into the dense digital forest and social media tropical underbrush we all inhabit nowadays – meandering through the various Facebook combat zones, aligning with allies, fighting off foes, reading "war reports" from our various news feeds ("our side" is always winning, or so we're told), connecting with family and friends, swinging from on-line vine to vine like internet Tarzans, posting the occasional primal scream to announce that we are the would-be kings and queens of virtual space.

As with any jungle, there are rules for survival in Cleveland's Greyhound station.

Those rules particularly apply at 3 am.

Always carry yourself with an aura of strength. Be vigilant and take note of your surroundings. Always observe people's body language from a distance and try sensing their intent. If your body language doesn't reflect confidence, strength and the willpower of a fighter, you are an easy prey.

As Tahir Shah said in House of the Tiger King, "The forest did not tolerate frailty of body or mind. Show your weakness, and it would consume you without hesitation."

One who understood the rules was a hard-looking middle-aged woman who sat in the far corner of the Greyhound Station waiting area. Her back to the wall away from the doors. Though she was traveling alone, she sat on a bench near a group of college students. She wore a large, puffy, black jacket which made her look larger. Her black boots were made of dull plastic and had shreds of what remained of grey fuzzy rings at the tops by her ankles. She wore loose black sweatpants which had white stains from the salt the city uses to melt snow. Her small carry-on luggage, also black with a broken wheel, was hard between her legs. She folded her arms across the top of her luggage handles and sat motionless.

Her bus was supposed to board in 15 minutes but hadn't yet arrived.

She sat there perfectly still. Impassive, as though in a Zen state. Or deaf. The occasional noises from the buses, announcements, people walking by – no stimulus evoked the slightest response. Invisible in the open. Even her eyes were hidden behind Black sunglasses. Wearing those indoors at 3 am.

As camouflaged in the open as a stick bug.

The three college-aged students, two young men and a young woman, were dressed hipster standard. One young man, around 5 feet, ten inches tall and very lean, had a curly brown beard which tressed in front down to his waist like Bizzaro-land Rapunzel. He was light-skinned and, as Clevelanders of that pigmentation tend to look that time of year, his shade was almost bluish-pale from lack of sun.

He wore an old Black leather jacket, over-sized Black-rimmed glasses, a multi-colored, African-style, Kofia hat, big tan construction boots, and Black sweat pants that looked remarkably similar to those worn by the middle-aged Zen woman who sat nearby. He was standing, with one boot on the wooden bench, holding his phone with one hand, as expertly and casually as an experienced smoker holds a cigarette.

He peered into the phone he was holding, looking like he was doing something clever and unknowable, but every so often would unobtrusively look about with his eyes, barely moving his head … left, right, behind.…

The small group's sentry.

His larger male companion, whose olive-coloring was more Mediterranean-looking, wore gaudy red skinny jeans with turned-up hem, blue, untied Doc Martins, a denim shirt-jacket tucked into the pants, Black gloves without finger-tips (by design), and a simple Asian-style pendant around his neck with a long, leather cord.

His hair was in a simple, slick, tussled quiff, and his handlebar moustache was perfectly waxed, shaped and coiffured, even though the rest of his face looked like it hadn't been shaved in two days. Two days exactly.

He didn't wear a hat.

This young man had just put out a cigarette even though he was sitting directly underneath one of the many "No Smoking" signs posted in the area. The large woman acting as security guard behind the desk was much too bored and fighting sleep to care, even though one couldn't help but notice this second young man.

Some jungle creatures don't feel the need for camouflage or to hide – in fact, quite the opposite.

The group's alpha.

The young woman with them was ebony-colored with high cheekbones. Her color almost perfectly matched the dark brown on the leather seats, although her flawless skin was spared the wear and tears of the furniture.

She was wearing an unbuttoned, oversized (much) plaid green flannel shirt which covered her hands, a band t shirt from two decades before she was born, a black bucket hat, a pair of steel-blue, beat-up Converse shoes, tight, tight Black skinny jeans with holes above the knees, and a black leather jacket with the sleeves rolled up to the elbows. Her eyes were shaped like Cleopatra's, only hers had even more makeup.

She seemed to talk, and think, and laugh, broadly, yet as if always in un-hearable magic whispers. Her eyes were always up and looking somewhere else, as though she had just recognized someone she knew from across the room.

The group's mate to be protected. Also, the group's

huntress.

Around and around the Greyhound jungle, as in the savannah, each had niched themselves into a spot, a jungle territory – a role to play out in the otherwise risky theater of traveling by bus.

Over there, four young African-American boys sat together not saying a word, looking tough. A picture of them would make the perfect cover for a rap album.

By the door, a large, nervous, mostly-bald fat man was either chatting quietly to himself or on a phone. It didn't matter. His "conversation" seemed to be focused on the injustice of evolution and how teaching it is what causes all the racism in the world. He also couldn't understand why he wasn't finding others who had evolved like him, which would agitate him until he reminded himself that it didn't matter because he was the only one who knew the secret. That would make him laugh, but only for a short time before he would return to the topic of finding the missing link. That would solve everything.

He paced back and forth as he talked. Three steps this way. Three steps that way.

Usually, crazy ones are left alone.

In the background, a surreal medley of songs from the waiting room in hell were pouring over the space, covering it like an itchy blanket. "Song, sung, blue, everybody knows one…". The sound system was blurry, which gave the audial atmosphere a hypnotic feel, like muffled static. Or a baby crying in another room, but dulled by layers of walls and far enough away that it still wouldn't keep you awake.

Introduced into this sonic wave-pattern of distant, sleepy nightmares were the sounds of garbage cans being jostled – like what you might hear in a backyard if your trash were being inspected by racoons. And, just like racoons, the garbage can rustler in the Greyhound station was also trying to be quiet, and was also unsuccessful in doing so.

The eyes of the jungle pivoted almost imperceptivity toward the source of the noise, yet if someone were looking through a video camera they'd have to zoom in to notice any shifting of eyeballs at all.

What the Greyhound jungle-dwellers saw was completely unremarkable. A homeless man going through the trashcans. His distinctive plumage immediately identified him in the urban jungle. Like some of the others in room, the homeless man who'd just entered was also wearing sweatpants, only his had elastic straps at the ankles – a style that had long since been unavailable in stores.

They were, or at least originally were, the same grey color and design that a 9th grade wrestling coach doubling as a gym teacher might have worn… in 1978. Perhaps, they were even the exact same sweatpants owned by that gym teacher/wrestling coach long ago, who wore them every day to school along with an ever-present whistle around his neck.

The homeless-looking man's sweatpants were spotted and speckled now, streaked and stained with blots and patches of black, brown, yellow and white. The elastic at the ankles and waist had long since expired, and his pants sagged. In fact, everything about him seemed to sag, as though his melting spirit were embodied, expressed, and played out in his physical visage.

It was hard to tell if he were wearing underwear, not that anyone would look so closely to determine for sure. Some material seemed to be covering the parts of his butt that hung above his sagging sweats – material that seemed to have originally been a red plaid (maybe?)

He seemed to have layers of multiple sweatshirts on, none of which were complete, as though he were shedding sweatshirts, like a snake sheds its skin. His color pattern resembled a car that had been rebuilt from junkyard parts and now had mismatched fenders.

A brown sweatshirt covered his right arm, a yellow sweatshirt his chest and most of his left arm. From the elbow down on his left arm, a greyish layer covered him, and across his back were remnants of what might have once been an orange blanket, but now just hung from his shoulders like Super Beggard's cape.

He staggered about from trashcan to trashcan, from waste bin to bin, salvaging for recyclable treasures, or perhaps a discarded something to eat, muttering to himself every step of the way that he'd better be quiet.

"Shtop making such a rack..racket ol' sod. You'll find yourself in hock with the ol' Bill." He would shush himself…over and over again extolling himself to be quiet while he sorted through society's discards –

discards like himself, that might extend his life another day, or perhaps to bring something less stark and gloomy.

He appeared to find a hat, stained and torn, in one of the bins. It said "Witness" on it. He put it on, wiped his face, looked about guiltily, took it off, and put it in the garbage bag he slung over his shoulder.

The security guard, who was due for a break, walked past the homeless man and asked him a question

"Just pickin' up a coupla' cans, mum, and I'll be on me way?"

She stood there, considered everything including her full bladder, took a whiff, flinched, and went on break.

And, so racoon-like, he staggered unsteadily along, like the many bottom-dwellers of society that have their own unwanted niche in the jungle.

Scavenger.

The rest of the neighborhood in the jungle eased from alert and went back to their wary commuter coma, each in turn, resuming their role as "non-prey."

Only one man in the room was still on alert. A man who was always on alert. Had lived his whole life on high alert, especially so since the incident.

He seemed to have somehow found a shadow in the room. Or created one. A tightly wound and tightly packed man. Hard and hardened. Leaning against a post in the corner. His head was facing a bit to the right and his Cleveland Browns baseball cap was low over his eyes. He seemed intent on a Scene magazine, one of the alternative free weeklies that occupy space in the few remaining newspaper bins.

But, he had no interest in the latest concert news. No, his focus was on escape. Getting out of town. Now. Today. Before he was caught.

He was clad in sheep's clothing. A worn black suitcoat that still had some life left, a white dress shirt, untucked and not too badly stained, faded jeans that had once been designer, dress shoes that looked okay so long as one didn't look too closely at the heels – they represented the best the local charities could put together as "interview clothes."

Only his over-stuffed, military-looking duffle bag was out of place for his guise as "casual business traveler" in this jungle. There was one other feature of his, however, that was also … out of place.

Out of face.

Discordant.

Or, at least it would seem discordant be for those rare individuals who would fight through their fear enough to look for it – to see it. A frightening feature and most unsettling. Like Medusa's hair – more safely gazed in reflection.

 A human's face is largely symmetric – similarly shaped, if not quite identical, from one side to the other.

This individual's face, however, had a feature most asymmetric. Although it was largely obscured by posture, positioning, and clothing, a jagged red line – like a visual expression of hatred and anger – sprawled across this individual's face from the corner of his mouth nearly to his right ear.

Like a panther – a black panther hiding in forest bushes – his true wolf's nature was invisibly hidden in the corner of the Greyhound station. Also hidden was an unknown truth – several really … this unobtrusive man could, and would, kill any other person in the room if there were the slightest chance that person might stand in the way of his escaping.

His bus was scheduled to board in ten minutes.

The jungle had only one member moving now. Going from can to can, gathering urban driftwood treasures, the homeless man meandered and muttered along with a strange efficiency, as though he'd walked this circuit before, perhaps many times, and each trash container took him along in a specific direction, like Balthasar, Melchior, and Gaspar following a special star, along a trail of refuse, and his path seemed to be pulling him along, pulling him along as destiny will…

… in the general direction of a non-descript business traveler reading a Scene magazine in the corner.

41

A Facebook page was created earlier the same day. It had one post. That post read:

"I am the Other.

Everyone dies the same. Everyone's blood is red. If it takes fear to bring us to understand that – if the streets need to run red to bring us together – to stop hating each OTHER over our differences – then the Other will be the last other and bring us together … by opening up our secret innards and paint those streets red... red that will run … together….

We need to stop fearing the other – those that are different colors, religions, orientations, political views, or countries.

Human beings weren't made for this – fearing the other.

It is obvious now, only one thing will bring us together – ONE Other.

If you must choose to fear an other, then I will be The Other that unifies fools in one collective fear.

I am the Other. You can stop building walls…

…or you will die behind them.

I am the Other.

That is all."

The Facebook page might have gone unnoticed. It

had no other posts or friends. It did have, however, one photograph. A photograph of a certain assistant district attorney that had been strangled in the park. A photograph that could only have been taken by someone who had been on the scene – been on the scene before the police got there.

The page got 487,000 views in the first three hours before Facebook took it down. It even got 23,000 likes, along with millions of screen captures.

The next week, Neighborhood watch groups in Cleveland tripled. Across the country, non-profit Community Guardian Escort (CGE) services blossomed. The app for the network of CGEs was becoming more common than Uber.

42

The homeless-looking man at the Greyhound station continued his trash can farming. Stumbling, swaying, staggering along, shuffling, his hands jittery and shaking, leaving behind a trail of waste paper and random refuse on the floor in his wake.

"Mustn't make a sound, ol' sod" he muttered to himself. "Shhhh, be quiet or you'll be getting' ya'self in troubles, in troubles agin', ol' sod, yar youz will, in troubles, troubles…" Along the trail of cans he crookeded along, connecting the dots forward to the final cans – the cans in the corner – the cans in the corner beside a hard-looking man, leaning against the wall, reading a magazine.

Twenty feet away from the man reading the magazine. Fifteen feet. The homeless-looking man wavered back and forth, barely able stay atop his feet, but no matter how far he staggered, he would somehow find a way to right himself, like a ship in stormy seas cast about in invisible waves. He didn't so much walk a line, as tack, like a sailboat traveling against the wind.

Now, ten feet…five… and the homeless-looking man made a funny-looking hop, two hops, and hollered "I'm drunk! Can you help a feller out??". The scarred man reading the magazine turned around but it was too late – the homeless-looking man tossed his treasure bag of trash into the air at the face of the man in the corner, gracefully leaped, and closed the remaining distance between the two.

The man in the corner deflected the trash bag projectile with his left arm, but he was a split-second too late. While the light bag was harmless in itself, it did serve its purpose. It distracted long enough for the homeless-looking man to grab the other's right wrist with his own right wrist, and place his left arm into the armpit of the man who had been reading a magazine only seconds before.

Simultaneously, in a way that had been rehearsed thousands of times before, the homeless-looking man remained close, and pivoted behind, pulled on the wrist, rotated the wrist forward, and drove his target's arm downward.

This straight-arm takedown maneuver bent the scarred man over, but he instantly responded by driving his right foot atop the left foot of his attacker. The homeless-looking man howled, but even though he didn't let go, his balance was affected ever so slightly – affected enough for the scarred one, even from a bent-over position, to deliver a body-blow with his left fist.

Oof!

The homeless-looking man lost his grip but not his determination. He started to assume a fighting stance, but his baggy clothes were ill-fitting for fighting, which delayed his stance just long enough for the scarred one to deliver a kick to his groin.

Combined with the previous blow to the gut, the homeless-looking man felt like he was underwater – he could barely breathe! The scarred one, sensing vulnerability, landed a right and a left to his attacker's face, which sent him to the ground.

The jungle dwellers around were excited, agitated, and alarmed!

"Fight! Fight!" the four African-American youths gleefully shouted out and stood up to get a better look.

The fat man by the door stopped pacing and began loudly lamenting the unfortunate evolution of fighting. "Darwin did this! Darwin! That motherFUCKER!"

The hard-looking middle-aged woman sitting on the booth was still as a statue.

In the dreamy, insipid, background of bland sonic

oatmeal, The Girl From Ipanema played on – the 1964 version by Astrud Gilberto & Stan Getz.

> *"When she walks, she's like a samba*
> *That swings so cool and sways so gentle that*
> *When she passes, each one she passes goes…"*

The scarred man, enraged that his plan to remain invisible in the jungle was ruined by this human garbage, leaped atop the homeless-looking man.

That was a mistake.

Even as the man he was now fighting for his life against was diving atop him, the homeless-looking man had assumed a ju-jitsu posture with his back to the ground. He wrapped up the diving man, catching him between his legs, and assumed control from the bottom – now pummeling him with vicious blows to the top man's throat and temples!

The scarred one managed, in full rage, to create enough distance to raise up a knee, which again landed home in the groin of the homeless-looking man.

This second blow to every man's soft spot left him in agony with swirling, twinkling lights spinning around his head. He released his grip with his legs and the scarred one was able to get to his feet first.

The scarred one landed several kicks to the ribs of the homeless-looking man, and stomped his head, like a professional wrestler. The scarred one grinned and began plotting targets. He was going to enjoy this.

From a dreamy place of half-consciousness, laying there

saturated in pain, the homeless-looking man had an image flash before his eyes. An image of what had been a beautiful, committed, idealistic assistant district attorney left slaughtered in North Royalton's Metroparks.

Somehow summoning a source of strength from the deepest reaches of his soul, he managed to raise his right leg just as the next stomp was coming, he managed to straighten it like a board…and now, it was his foot that struck gonads.

By now, the intensity of the combat was starting to take the fun out of watching what the rest of the jungle originally thought was just a random fight amongst bums. No, the ferocity of each man's calculated, vicious attacks started to frighten the bystanders who wondered what they should do to keep someone from getting killed… or if they should do anything.

The hipster girl looked at her big Arab friend, which was the cue. The trio stood up and trotted over to help the scarred one defend himself from his homeless attacker.

As they scampered over, the homeless-looking man somehow found a second wind and hobbled to his feet.

He again grabbed control of the other's wrist with his outside arm, and taking advantage of the scarred one's momentum, pulled the arm back towards his body. The scarred one instinctively pulled his arm back, bending it at the elbow, at which point, the homeless-looking man moved his inside hand over the other's upper arm, under his forearm, while grabbing the outside arm in a figure-four lock. He rotated his body towards the scarred man, driving him backward and downward.

The scarred one, still shaken by the blow to the groin, rotated to the ground, forced to the prone position. At that point, the homeless-looking man used his forearm against the shoulder joint, placing downward pressure, and driving the wrist upward to maintain control.

"Hey, you bum! Leave that guy alone!" The slender hipster with the prodigious beard was fast approaching, emboldened by the presence of his larger friend, only a few feet behind him.

"I mean it, you drunken psycho! Either you let that guy up, or we're going to kick your ass!"

The striking ebony hipster chick stood behind her large Arab friend and her eyes danced and twinkled in excitement, like a mother lion might beam watching her cub's first kill.

> *"Tall and tan and young and lovely*
> *The girl from Ipanema goes walking and*
> *When she passes, I smile but she doesn't see, doesn't see…"*

The hipster trio, now surrounding the two men on the ground, the one controlling the other, waited before attacking to see if their verbal orders would be obeyed.

The homeless-looking man, for the first time during this entire theater of violence, began to look about desperately. The security guard was outside, leaning against the wall, smoking a cigarette.

> *"But I watch her so sadly*
> *Porque tudo to triste*

Yes, I would give my heart gladly…"

The four African-American toughs bounced over in case backup with street combat experience were needed. Now, the two men on the ground were surrounded by the seven, the four toughs and three hipsters.

The fat man by the door was complaining again, only now in a full bellow – an abdominal yell, echoing throughout the lobby like from an opera singer, "In two days, I'll be evolved beyond this too. Evolved beyond this too. Fuck Darwin! Fuck On the Origin of Species! Fucking intelligent design is where all this is headed, and all you DEVOLVED assholes will be left behind! Take RAPTURE, motherfuckers!!!"

> *"Por causa do amor*
> *She just doesn't see*
> *Nem olha para mim*
> *She never sees me*
> *Por causa do amor…"*

The homeless-looking man raised up, and delivered a knee to the ribs of the man he was controlling.

"That's it motherfucker!" bearded hipster came forward and cocked his fist.

The homeless-looking man, having stunned his foe momentarily, was able to release one hand long enough to reach into his pocket and take out a slender, leather rectangle.

"Fuck you" the bearded hipster sprang forward, about to strike, his large Arab friend inches behind now.

"Fuck you!" the homeless-looking man hollered back, opening and flashing his worn, leather, rectangle.

"I'm a cop! And this man's under arrest for murder!"

43

"Why the hell didn't you just shoot the motherfucker?" Johnson was making a rare appearance outside the Berea Batcave. His partner, about to receive widespread adulation, was lying in a hospital bed, looking badly beaten.

"Believe me, Johnson, about two seconds in, I was asking myself the same question." Jack Wharton was happy to have gotten his man. He was happy to still be alive. He was also happy as a result of the pharmaceutical cocktail the attending physician had prescribed for pain.

"Look, dude, your Navy SEAL days are long, long behind you. You need to look in the mirror sometimes. Your six pack is now more like a case. What the hell were you thinking?"

Navy SEAL. How long ago had that been? A Jewish pencil-necked kid with a rough upbringing trying to prove something. Trying to prove something to himself. Trying to do something that would have made his parents proud…if they'd lived long enough to see his son graduate.

It flashed back to him unexpectedly. His long-time partner, Johnson, fading away replaced by the images, the hope, the desperation, the brotherhood, the pain, pain,

pain, the place a person can find that goes beyond determination, beyond will, far, far beyond physical strength.

A place of "Mind Leads. Body Follows." A place where some purpose, some all-encompassing purpose, becomes a soul's anchor in the storm, the singular focus. To do it for… dad? Mom? Society? Yourself? Your country? The brothers to your left and right?

That was part of it.

But, it mostly just "was." A place that one finds in their core and then lashes themselves to the mast. A place beyond them, that somehow allows them to endure, to sustain… to do things they never thought they ever could. Things they never thought they ever would.

A purpose.

A purpose.

Maybe, something deeply rooted from a long-forgotten childhood experience that had grown inside as a painful seed, like a pearl inside a clam. Maybe, something about what they want to believe they see when they look in the mirror. Maybe, something from heaven – a limitless source of strength from an old man with a gray beard in the sky.

But, whatever the sustaining, driving force is, it comes from outside, or feels like it. From some other place. And allows one to endure. To continue.

To not give up. To be committed.

The 24-week Basic Underwater Demolition/SEAL

school (BUD/S). Only about 1% of those who enter BUD/S training complete it. Every day, every exercise, the trainers reminding everyone "all you got to do is ring the bell, pussies! Ring the bell and you get to go back to just being a regular, old Navy sailor…like everyone else. It's easy. Just go ring the bell.

"Because, if you don't…if you DON'T then I am going to fuck…you…UP!

"How does that wave feel, pussies? How does that wave FEEL!?!? Cuz, here comes another one."

Did they WANT you to quit?

Jack Wharton never reflected on this experience. Damn Johnson. Reminded him of times he was generally successful forgetting.

He thought now of the night gear exchange – swapping breathing masks with other sailors that have totally blacked out underwater. To totally black out underwater himself, and awaken with someone else's mask providing oxygen to breathe. To return to life.

The 28-week SEAL qualification training.

Advanced cold weather training.

Close quarters combat training.

Surf passage training at Coronado.

News that his parents had died in a car crash. No, they wouldn't see him finish.

His graduation. One tear.

Then, six months later. The psychological examination.

"Why are they picking me out for that, Sarge?"

Didn't every sailor drink?

Washed out. Honorably. "Mental Instability Disability."

Sealed records. And, the path this Cleveland cop had taken to this hospital bed had one more experience to lock away, shutter up in the attic. Another seed. Perhaps, another pearl. With all the rest.

"Yah. I guess my old fellow snake eaters would be disappointed. Seems I fight like an old shoe nowadays." Jack had returned from his dream reminisce, which in truth only lasted for maybe 5 seconds, but felt much, much longer.

That brought Johnson back into focus.

"Tell you what, though," Jack continued, "that guy had moves they didn't teach in BUD/S! He should open his own fighting dojo – call it street-rat style."

"Why the hell didn't you shoot? Or, just call for back up?"

"Didn't want to start a gunfight in the Greyhound. I also thought I'd be able to restrain him myself pretty easy if I surprised him. Didn't want him getting on a bus waiting for backup. Didn't want to have to kill the guy, which I knew I'd have to if I pulled out my gun."

A picture returned in Jack's head – of a certain young Assistant District Attorney – a picture that had appeared during his battle in the bus depot. "And, I wanted him alive."

"Ok, hero. Look what you got for going all Rambo. What made you think he'd be at the bus station anyway?"

Jack had been trying to answer that question himself.

"I told you I had a hunch. Something. Not sure what. Just woke up and felt like our boy was about to flee. Tonight. The next night."

"A hunch, Jack? You know, I think hunches are bullshit."

"Well, I did grow up with the guy, maybe we're connected." Jack didn't like to think that, but it came out. "it wasn't all a hunch, though. Your profiling had predicted that taking a bus was one of the more likely avenues of escape he would choose. So, it was a hunch… combined with your research! Looks like you're a hero, too, pard'ner!"

Jack was only vaguely aware that he had made something resembling a smile for the first time in a long, long time.

"Oh no, hero! I specifically put your name to that profile report, and your name only! I'm invisible in this work for a reason. You won't make a hero out of me!" Johnson was serious and Jack knew it. "You so much as bring up my name, and I'll make it look like you're deliberately deflecting. Don't piss people off. Just be the hero. Our town needs a hero."

Jack rarely was able to beat his partner in these "debates."

"Hey, I am proud of you, dude. I wonder, though, about a guy who's that great at pretending they're a homeless guy, but you got your man, dude. You did it!"

Jack didn't mind losing this part of the debate.

"Well, visiting hours are about to start, so I gotta' go. You need anything…" and, even though it was cliché, Jack knew it was sincere.

With that, Johnson disappeared, seconds before Jack's first visitor of the day. It wouldn't be his last.

In walked a hard-looking African-American man in uniform, looking harder than ever. Looking like the kind of guy if you punched him in the face, your fist would hurt worse. In walked Cleveland's Chief of Police, Calvin D. Williams.

Alone.

"Hey Chief! Thanks for coming by," Jack wheezed out as best he could, lying there with cracked ribs … grateful for the artificial good cheer provided by his prescribed pharmaceuticals.

44

Inside a in a place that some might consider the closest thing to hell in Ohio, another man was recovering from wounds suffered during a vicious battle in a downtown bus station. Only this person's recovery wasn't supported by a stream of honoring dignitaries expressing gratitude. Nor was his every medical need attended to by an eager brigade of comely young nurses. There were no massages, warm sponge baths, congratulatory calls, or comforting pharmaceutical cocktails to ease this injured soul's suffering.

No, this person's recovery was taking place about an hour's drive outside Cleveland, in a city called Youngstown. And rather than being housed in a world-class medical facility like the Cleveland Clinic, this person was confined inside the state's most secure prison, the Ohio State Penitentiary.

The Ohio State Penitentiary houses many of Ohio's most deviant and violent predators. Meals are shuttled to cells in boxes. Guards carefully monitor the inmates who are allowed to leave their cells, and keep them moving and separated.

The prison is divided into two sections: the super-maximum and the maximum blocks. In the super-max, the state's worst inmates – about 120 — live in cells about the size of a parking space. They stay there 23 hours a day. If they want to exercise outside, they can go into a fenced-in area that has a screen above them.

It was inside one of these super-max accommodations that this certain prisoner was placed to wait. This was to be his place of recuperation. He was angry but resigned. Pain he knew as a familiar companion.

He accepted his companion's presence like someone might learn to tolerate a nagging spouse. Or like maybe a whale comes to accept a crusting of barnacles that attach themselves to its body. He didn't even have to try to block it out, for what good that might do.

Pain simply was. Always had been. An unwelcome, unwanted companion to be sure, but it wasn't going anywhere. There. Here. With him.

Before coming here, he'd actually spent an hour in some sort of state medical office, where he was stitched up – without any topical analgesic – had a bag of frozen peas applied to his aching groin for maybe 15 minutes, and had an old white guy with one of those old-fashioned mirrored head bands twist his arms and bend his legs, before proclaiming that "nothing seems broken." This "doctor" had yellow teeth and his breath and clothes smelled of cigarettes.

He did not receive any x-rays although he was given two Advil.

Normally, anyone arrested in Cleveland's downtown Greyhound station, as he was, would be taken straight to the Cleveland City Jail. Located on 1300 Ontario Street, it's less than a mile away – simply go north on East 13th, up to St. Claire, take a left, and you're there in five minutes.

This prisoner's journey, however, was special. Governor John Kasich was wakened in the middle of the night to order a special journey for this special prisoner. And so, this one sat, under direct orders from the governor himself. In a special cell. In a special place. This involuntary guest with a very recognizable scar ... that so many people had been looking for.

This feral, monstrous animal, finally caught and placed in the most secure cage in the state of Ohio.

And, in this cage, he read a newspaper he'd picked up waiting for the stinky old man posing as a doctor to come in and put a bag of frozen peas on his tortured balls.

"LOCAL COP CAPTURES SUSPECT IN STRING OF TERRORISTIC MURDERS," the headline from the Cleveland Plain Dealer screamed in banner typeface. "Undercover hero prevails in dramatic bus terminal battle," read the sub-head. This one with the scar stared at the pictures. First, the picture of the arresting officer.

Heroic. Worn. Relieved. Beaming with pride blanketed in genuine humbleness. The kind of guy you'd like to see at the door to pick up your sister.

Then, an old mug shot of himself, taken after a prior arrest for public intoxication. He looked Hollywood typecast for psycho killer – the scar (of course), disheveled hair, bloodshot eyes that raged, various facial bruises he received, not during the arrest, mind you, but administered in a parking lot by "Cleveland's finest" on the way to the station.

He had been neither protected nor served on that day, but he had been photographed, and there he was, on the front page, looking like a guy already convicted and on his way to Ohio's next opportunity to botch a lethal injection at the Southern Ohio Correctional Facility in Lucasville.

He couldn't figure out how his life journey had led to this point. The shattered shards of the dismal, dreary menagerie of his past had never seemed to fit – they'd always seemed so misshapen and contorted. Deformed days connected, one by one, like bricks in a hideous house of mirrors wall with no door, windows, or exit.

Now that the disfigured pieces of a scarred life were busted apart, it didn't matter anyway how they once might have been whole. Because all the king's horses and all the king's men weren't going to be able to put the turd bricks of his shithouse existence back together again.

Was he born broken? Was he destined to be marked? Was he meant to be scarred, and to feel a need to hurt others who weren't?

Was he doomed at birth?

Does fate just decide to single individuals out, like a pigeon's prank, to shit on?

The pieces now didn't fit. It felt like he was encaged, not in a prison cell, but in a patchwork quilt of puzzle pieces from several different boxes – some fit and others looked like they didn't even belong – they couldn't possibly be put together.

The picture assembled from these random junkyard pieces didn't make sense.

He read the article in Cleveland's daily paper again.

"Jack Wharton…. Jack Wharton…." He muttered the name of the arresting officer to himself.

"Wait a minute." He thought to himself, mulling over how these mismatched puzzle pieces might be forced to fit together in a way that made some kind of mad sense. Wasn't that the name of that kid he grew up with?

That kike kid? ….yah.

"The Wart!"

"What the fuck. The Wart…" …and memory pieces came blinking into his mind and their shapes kept shifting and turning in his ruminations. One thing prisoners have in abundant wealth is time. Time to think. And, as he thought back on those days, and that Jewish kid in his Italian neighborhood, the pieces shifted over and over, and like a mental game of Tetris where the pieces changed shape on their way down, he played the game – spinning pieces this way, and then that way, to bring an image into focus.

And, he stared at the wall, and the puzzle pieces became whole.

And, he stared at the wall, and could see how the puzzle pieces would fit together in the future.

The near future.

And, his companion was there, and would be bringing friends.

That was the picture he saw.

In that cage.

Alone.

In a cell that was being given very special attention, in the super-max section of the Ohio State Penitentiary, in

Youngstown, Ohio.

It was eleven days before Christmas.

45

"So, you got a call from the president?!?" Johnson was almost never impressed, but there was a song of respect, and maybe a tinge of jealousy, in his voice.

Jack limped into the Berea Batcave kitchen and poured himself a tomato juice out of the fridge. He only put a short half-shot of vodka in a tall drink, came out into the actual Batcave central, and plopped down on the worn recliner like a king who'd returned from victorious war might triumphantly plop on his thrown. He took a gulp off his drink, and exhaled …. ahhhh.

"Yep."

"What'd he say?"

"That he was glad I was helping make America great again."

"No way. The president of the United States called my partner, Jack Wharton, in the hospital and told him he was part of making America great again?"

"Yep."

"Really?"

"Yep."

"What an asshole! What else did he say?"

"He went on for about 10 minutes about all the work he's doing to fight terrorists. The most victories of any president in history! Then, he said something about Muslims and working with law enforcement – like me and you buddy! – helping law enforcement fight Mexican gangs. Then, he said he hoped Cleveland would vote for him in the next election, and hung up."

"Amazing. So, you arrest Ray Cardibello, born and raised in Cleveland's Little Italy, and the president of the United States thanks you for helping fight Islamic Terrorists and Mexican gangs. What did you say?"

"I thanked him for his call and inspiring leadership."

"Inspiring leadership. You thanked him for inspiring leadership."

"Yep."

A full five seconds of silence.

Each man looked each other in the eye and blinked twice.

Then, uproarious laughter!!

"Oh my God! Jack! What the fuck! 'Inspiring leadership' God DAMN that's funny!! What did he say to that?"

"He said 'thank you.'"

"He said 'thank you'!! HAHAHA! 'Thank you! Oh, man, that is PRECIOUS! I'm dying! I can't breathe I'm laughing so hard!"

"Yep."

And Jack Wharton, hero, joined his long-time partner in a laugh that only buddies can really share.

"Goddamn, Jack! That's better than sex!", which set off another round of buddy laughs, this time while passing a flask now half-filled with Dewers.

"So, who else came and visited while you were in the hospital?"

"Damn near everyone, partner. I'm pissed at you, by the way, for your not letting me talk about your role in all this!"

"Never mind. Who else?"

"Well, the chief, of course. I almost thought he was going to cry at one point, but I think his tears were too scared to touch his face!"

"The chief, of course. One tough monkey."

"And, the mayor, his'oner Frank G. Jackson. He brought flowers."

"Did he put it on his city credit card?"

"I'd ask the florist, but I think we both know the answer."

More buddy laughs.

"The head of the union came by. He brought flowers too, and a box of cigars. Good ones!"

"Our union dues put to good use for a change. Was

the card signed Jeff or Steve – you know, those guys keep taking turns every year!"

Even more buddy laughs.

"Tons of media. Most of them, I just said I was too tired, but check who I wasn't too tired for... Kristi Capel!"

"The Fox news hottie!!? No way! What's she like?"

"A little self-absorbed, and not overly bright, but she smells like hungry roses! Really sped up my ... ah.. recovery!"

"Damn!"

"Got a ton of phone calls. Spoke with both Senator Brown and Senator Portman."

"What'd they want?"

"They both were pretty nice, actually. They each thanked me a million times and said if I ever need anything at all. Anything. Just give them a call. They both seemed like decent Joes."

"Okay. Who else?"

"Rachel Maddow called. She wanted to know if I thought our hostility toward immigrants and availability of guns made my job harder."

"What'd you tell her?"

"That I was just about to get some shots and had to go."

"What was the weirdest question you were asked?"

"I don't know if I can think of the weirdest, but I can tell you the one I heard the most often. Everyone wanted to know how I knew to stake out the bus station at just that time, in disguise."

"What'd you tell 'em?"

"Mostly, a version of the truth – hard work, profiling, process of elimination, hunch, combination of all of them. But, you know, partner, what I'm really thinking?"

"Nope. Tell me what you really think, Mr. Celebrity."

"I think there's a connection. A connection between people who grow up in the same 'hood together. Who see and feel the same things together as children, to where, even if you weren't close friends with them, you still have a common root, a root that keeps you on some same wavelength. Truth is, I just had a feeling. I woke up one day from some shitty dream I couldn't really remember, and it just kinda' came to me."

"You tell anyone that?"

"Nah. They'd think I was crazy. Mostly, I just played it off like humble Gary Cooper. P'shaw. Twern't nuthin'. Just lucky, ah' guess.'"

"Perfect! Now, you'll have to write a book!"

"Hoo boy! I just want for all this hoopla' to fade away so I can get back to just being a normal cop."

"Who says you were ever normal?"

"Ha. A. Ha. Hey, know what I've been thinking of doing, now that I'm a hero on a winning streak?"

"Afraid to ask. Go to Disneyland?"

"Call Mildred."

Johnson nearly did a spit-take.

"Mildred?!? What the fuck is WRONG with you? Why not just go the pound and ask if you can play with a rabid Pitbull?"

"Come on, now. What did Mildred ever do to you?"

"A 'tuh! You know I did everything I could to avoid her. But man, she not only took everything you had, she stole your soul along the way! Why the HELL would you look backward into that highway of pain again, anyway?"

"You know, PARTNER, I was married to her once. And, we had some… good times too…."

"Ok, I'm calling the hospital. Clearly, our hero boy's injuries include amnesia now. You don't remember her weekend 'knitting club' trips? What she called you? What she said about you to her friends? What she said about us to her friends? Three words. Don't. Do. It."

"Three words. Fuck. You…ummm…Twice! There. That's three. Look. We have mirrors in this place. Last checkup, my eyes were still 20/20. I can see what the mirror tells me clearly. I'm an old man with no hobbies, activities, or interests outside being a cop. I don't make clever conversation, I'm not good-looking, I'm not funny, I'm not rich. I'm a cop. And, there's not one woman in a hundred that can stand being with a cop who's just a cop. Mildred is one of them."

"You know, I could call a couple girls…"

"Thanks. But, I'm calling Mildred."

"Fuuuuuck."

Another five seconds of silence.

Two more blinks.

"Well, that's sure one helluva' way to try to make America great!"

One more buddy laugh, but Johnson's stopped just a bit shorter this time, and ended before Jack's.

46

Two days later, Jack and Mildred were in a Days Inn off Engle Road in Middleburg Heights – naked, happy, and spent. They'd been fucking like an asteroid was about to strike the earth.

47

"You know, Vanessa Altuve was a friend of mine." Ray Cardibello's court appointed attorney, Gary Stasky, Esquire, was making a point of whispering into his client's ear. "A good friend."

The two were walking, side by side, down the back hallway of the Carl B. Stokes United States Federal Courthouse. Located on 801 West Superior Avenue and named after the first African-American mayor of a major American city, the Courthouse's architecture, according to its webpage "is meant to project the prominence of justice in democracy, as well as the dignity, traditions, and civic pride associated with federal courthouses throughout the country."

Cardibello, together with his esteemed legal counsel, was taking the "private hallway route" dedicated to high-risk suspects on their way to trial. They were being escorted from their starting point at the Ohio Penitentiary cell in Youngstown – Cardibello's new home – by two of Cleveland's finest. Both of their police officer chaperones were big, Black, professional, and serious – personally hand-picked by the Chief for this detail. Cardibello was dressed in jailhouse orange, his hands chained to a belt around his waist and his feet shackled so he had to walk in short little bunny steps.

His attorney – the one whispering sweet nothings in his ear as the four men walked to the courtroom – looked like a lawyer from Hollywood central casting. Power suit (gunpowder grey), power hair (dark and slicked back), power shoes (with a professional polish), power tie (solid red), power stance (head up, elbows out), power physique (long and lean), and power face (stern, like a ship's captain in a storm).

Today was to be Cardibello's first appearance in court, simply to enter a plea.

Cardibello had only met his attorney an hour earlier, and the sum total of their discussion about his "defense" focused on the unlikelihood of an insanity plea succeeding in Ohio.

"Only 15% of the 1.36% of murder cases in which an insanity plea are entered result in acquittal," his attorney gleefully reported. "I wouldn't want my life depending on an event that occurred in .23% of cases."

His attorney never asked if his client was guilty. Nor did he seem to care, all that much.

"I saw pictures of what you did to her, you walking bag of shit", the honorable Gary Stasky, Esquire, continued with his whispered conversation. "You are fucked."

Cardibello just grinned. He'd been having these sorts of lovely conversations since he was arrested.

As he had been doing from the beginning, he kept these conversations one-sided, and didn't say a word.

Walking into the courtroom from the private door in the back felt like a famous actor making their first entrance in a theatrical play. He could feel the intense heat of spotlight.

His appearance buzzed the expectant audience with electricity. The emotions in the room were like a musical performance, an orchestra of feelings everyone played and heard together – over there was the percussion of anticipation, over here were the horns of fascinating curiosity. The strings section of hatred started overlaying the shock of the piano chords. The revulsion and primal notes of revenge were guitar riffs like something Jimmy Page might play.

The courtroom concert performers consisted of: friends and relatives of the Other's victims; national and local press (jostling for position like newborn puppies scrambling for the teats); lookie-Lous and courtroom groupies; and a random scrabble of law enforcement investigators that had led the charge in finding "the Other." Each contributed to the symphony in the room, emoting in a collective cacophony of passion that radiated and echoed around in reverent silence.

You can always "feel" a courtroom – the lasting echoes of emotions never fully fade away from the walls.... they're absorbed and resonate forever like a tuning fork of pain that never stops ringing.

Cardibello could "hear" all of this – was engulfed in the discordant emotional crescendo building in the room the moment he first stepped into the court. Of course he could. The "sound" of hate is easy to hear ... when it's aimed at you.

"All rise, for the honorable Patricia Gaughan."

Everyone in the room rose. Cardibello never had an opportunity to sit, having been marched directly to the defendant's table. No one indicated he should sit, and he'd already learned to expect consequences for doing anything, no matter how slight, that he wasn't directed to do. So, he'd just stood there while everyone else sat, exposed and visible so everyone could focus their hate rays right down to his soul, like a magnifying glass's focus burning an ant on the sidewalk.

What no one could know, however, is that all this theater of hate accomplished was to amuse their target who, truly, was a man without conscience. A man whose soul hadn't been sold, but was missing at birth. He was born man incomplete. Sans soul.

He was also a man who saw the world clearly. And, he'd already seen his own future, most clearly of all, at a moment when the puzzle pieces came together in his cell.

"Mr. Stasky, you and your client may approach the bench." The defendant, and his wonderfully supportive, court-appointed, power attorney approached the bench side-by-side, looking like young, slim Perry Mason accompanying a rabid, human Pitbull, bunny-hopping along in orange.

"Mr. Raymond G. Cardibello, today you stand before the court accused of the crime of Domestic Terrorism under 18 U.S. Code § 2331. How do you plea?"

The right Honorable Judge Patricia Gaughan, the first female Chief Judge of the Northern District of Ohio, wasn't from central casting. She looked like, in another setting, she might have been considered almost attractive. Mid-forties, blonde, blue eyes, high cheekbones, smile wrinkles around her eyes – in another day, she was what might have been called "a handsome woman." Not pretty, really, but an honest, strong face.

Five seconds of silence.

"Mr. Cardibello, how do you plea?"

Pretty, almost… in another place.

In this place, this courtroom – her courtroom – she didn't look pretty. Those blue eyes, rather than possessing a charming sparkle, instead were a pair of cold steel x-ray traps – like she had an internal measuring tape that instantly saw through and sized up everyone they examined. Her blonde hair was pulled back so fiercely that it reminded of the corsets worn by Victorian women.

Five more seconds.

"Mr. Stasky, is your client prepared to enter a plea at this time? As this is a potential capital offense, if a plea is not entered, a plea of not guilty will be entered on his behalf."

In this place, this courtroom – her courtroom … she looked like the strictest, meanest 6th grade math teacher in the world and everyone else on the planet was her student. And, that's how she made everyone else feel.

Everyone.

Though he'd never admit it, he wouldn't deny it either – even Cleveland's Chief of Police dreaded testifying in the courtroom of the Honorable Patricia Gaughan.

"Mr. Stasky, your client's plea," and Gary Stasky, Esquire, feeling exactly like a 6th grader, began to answer…in a voice that sounded a bit like a 6th grader's.

"Your honor, my client pleads…"

"Wart!" Cardibello interrupted in a bellow – the first words coming from his mouth since he was arrested.

"Mr. Stasky!" the intimidating judicial scold on the bench began, most unamused, "what is the meaning of…."

"WART!" Cardibello repeated, in an opera singer's baritone that vibrated off the walls and drowned out the emotional harmonies that he'd felt when he entered the room.

"WART!" he bellowed again. "I plead WART! WART, WART, WART, WARRRRT!" The hand-picked police escorts had already grabbed the suspect by both arms and had him immediately in their complete physical control, but he kept bellowing "WART! I will talk to the Wart! I have nothing to say to ANY motherfucker – excuse me, your honor – any honorable mother-fucker, except the Wart! You want to know anything? ANYTHING?!? I'm only talking to the WART!"

The two cops had already begun dragging their charge out of the courtroom and back out the door they'd entered only moments before. The suspect's attorney simply watched, along with everyone else, from the bench.

Once the boisterous accused murderer had been bustled out by two of Cleveland's finest, the right honorable Judge Patricia Gaughan said "a plea of not guilty will be entered on behalf of Mr. Raymond Cardibello."

The right honorable Judge Patricia Gaughan momentarily raised her right eyebrow at Gary Stasky, Esquire,

Majorem Dei Gloriam."

"To the greater glory of God."

Riley wore a cross around his neck with those words. And he had one tattoo. A St. Ignatius Wildcat. Every day after his shift, he attended mass at St. Ignatius of Antioch Church on 10205 Lorain Ave. He'd first stop off at Bobby O's – a "workingman's sports bar" open at 5:30 am. Drink two pints of Bud, have ham and eggs for breakfast, and go to mass.

Same exact routine.

Every day for 27 years.

On this day, he crossed another square off the calendar – exactly 39 days until retirement. He had a Hawaiian shirt hanging from the door which he was going to wear on his last day. He already had plane tickets to Hawaii for later that same day. Just he and his wife of 47 years, Katherine Marie Riley.

Thirty nine days away now.

Riley, of course, knew every square inch of the plant. Knew the places the kids would try to sneak in. Knew the places where the homeless would try to sleep. Knew the places where the squirrels would come up and take a peanut from the hand of a familiar, friendly face.

Because protecting water, after all, is an important responsibility, one O' Toole took very seriously – even if the most threatening encounter he'd ever actually experienced was a loose Pitbull.

He saw himself as a first responder, tasked with "protecting America." Proud Wildcat. Protecting America.

Half hour left in his shift. One final walk around the facility. Check the doors, register at the electronic checkpoints throughout the grounds (to document he'd actually made his rounds), record any observations for the day shift, toss a few peanuts at the squirrels, and then off to Buddy O's.

Riley always alternated his route, as per regulation, so as to prevent anyone trying to scope out the facility from predicting his whereabouts at any particular point in time. Today, he began his final inspection by exiting first from the east door.

Riley walked down the stairs to the lawn with a bit of spring in his step. It was going to be a nice sunny day with a projected high of 50 degrees – warm for Cleveland in December. He felt he was still pretty spry for a man a month away from retiring. He looked upward to the sky and enjoyed the moon, whose sheen was only beginning to lose its luster to the first hints of sunrise. He liked the moonlight on his face.

Something.

In the corner of his eye.

Something moved.

Riley knew every leaf, blade of grass, and pebble on the grounds. His mind's radar discovered something out of place. A blip. Moving.

Had he been looking straight at it, he would likely have

missed it, but the corners of our eyes notice movement more keenly, and it was his eye's corner that registered movement.

Subtle movement, but it wasn't an animal moving. Moving in the tree-wooded area to the east.

No, someone – some person – was moving about. Likely a kid. Or homeless. Either way, the property is off grounds, and Riley took seriously his responsibilities to keep unauthorized entries off the grounds. He made sure everyone else took it seriously too.

It had rained lightly throughout the night. The grass was wet and the ground muddy, but someone out there – out there in those woods – was moving, and moving in a way that suggested they didn't want to be seen.

Out there in the woods. A homeless-looking man was moving. Moving secretively, like a spy, trying not to be seen.

Chief Security Inspector Patrick Halloran Riley, with his 17 years' experience on what he proudly called "the Force", the former and lifelong Wildcat, the devout Catholic 39 days from a much-deserved retirement…

…was about to investigate what was happening in those woods to the east.

50

"Wow. Home early, I see. Eight am. Impressive. Either a great night or an awful one, which was it?"

Johnson always seemed to turn up at the Berea Batcave whenever Jack Wharton expected him to, and today, for reasons known only to Johnson, there he appeared — first thing in the morning, sprawled out on the torn and worn recliner couch, already drinking an Irish coffee, looking over the day's reports.

Silence.

"Oh. That bad, huh? Sorry pard'ner." When two men have been together as long as Johnson and Wharton, it's not uncommon for words to be unnecessary.

"Well, you tell me. I got dumped, in a public place I had arranged to maybe propose. Yeah, I was more than just thinking of it. Was gonna' try to talk her into giving it another go. Even bought a ring.

"Part of this lovely breakup, she tells me that she just used me to try to re-launch her acting career. You must have seen her doing interviews yourself — she's on all the cable news, looking like a cross between Jill Lawrence and Malala Yousafzai. America's hot new crusader for equality and justice. She's radiating 'hire me' waves like a Van Gogh painting. And, you KNOW the offers are pouring in. She'll probably get someone to write a book and put her name as the author.

"While she's tearing my heart out of my body and holding it in her hand, a couple airheaded cuties come over and ask her for her autograph. Then, when I try to tell her how much I love her and get her to change her mind, she tells me what a lousy lover I am.

"To top it all off, during all this wonderful experience, in the background, a couple laughing hyena jackasses hit a Keno and are whooping it up like they just threw the winning touchdown in the Super Bowl! All with Michael Stanley playing, which I paid a dollar to hear."

Johnson did what he does best in such circumstances. Know enough to not say anything. Or ask any questions. Cops know all kinds of dark secret places where they can stay tucked inside all night.

"So, what have I missed while I was out having fun?" Wharton did what was his duty to eventually do – change the subject for the both of them.

"Well, your buddy Cardibello went all psycho in court."

"Oh. How so."

"Well, for starters, he didn't plead guilty or not guilty. He pleaded 'wart.'"

"He pleaded what?"

"Not what. 'Wart'"

"He pled 'wart."

"Yup."

"What the hell does that mean?"

"I think it has something to do with you. Wasn't that the nickname he had for you as a kid?"

"Cardibello pled me?!? How did that go? Who was the judge?"

"Well, there was a bit of a scene. Couple gorillas from the state pen dragged him out, all the while he's screaming that you're the only one he'll talk to. Took him out the back way, where he, uh… 'tripped' a few times.

"Oh, and the judge you ask? None other than Patty Gaughan."

"No way. He did this in front of Max Patty? How'd she take all that?"

"Not amused."

"Wish I could have seen all that, pard'ner. Sounds like a much better show than the one I was in last night."

"Well, you're heading back into this one. Chief wants you to call the office right away. Your childhood chum won't say a word to anyone. Just you. Not a word. Not even his own attorney, who I believe you know. Stasky?"

"Gary? Oh man! He used to be hot for Vanessa! How'd the court let that happen?"

"Max Patty. Anyway, the feds want to hear whatever's on this psycho friend of yours mind, so they're going to oblige him and so… you're being called into today's interrogation."

"Lovely. You got another one of those."

"Already made one for you, my man. Say, you look like you're limping worse today."

"Makes this drink even more important then. Here's to bitches and riches."

And, the two lifelong friends tinked glasses, and gulped down their shared, liquid breakfast.

51

Chief Security Inspector Patrick Halloran Riley, the former and lifelong Wildcat, knew every inch, nook, hideaway, secret passage, not so secret passage, and places in the fence where people would try to climb or cut their way into the Garrett A. Morgan Water Treatment Plant. He was pretty sure he just glimpsed a homeless guy sneaking around the wooded area bordering the eastern boundary of the plant, and it was his job – no, more than his job, his calling – to keep the plant providing safe drinking water to much of Greater Cleveland.

Homeless guys and drunk teens usually meant one thing – someone trying to sneak a pee into the finished water reservoir. Something about water, he'd learned long ago. People were always trying to either spit in it or pee in it, and usually, at the water treatment plant, it was the peeing that was the problem. What is it, he often wondered, about the instinctive attraction of water? And why, if you were of a mind to pee in water, would you go to all the trouble of sneaking in to pee in the water you drink?

He hadn't seen the homeless man since his initial glimpse. He scoured around the wooded area where he originally spotted the glimpse, but there was no trace. But his experience told him he had a "whizzer" on his hands, and so he laid his usual trap.

The water in the reservoir is only accessible from the outside through one of the air vents on top of twin geodesic domes that "cap" the water storage unit. Climbing those domes to access the vents at the top required agility and athleticism, and he was always amazed to see the various intoxicated, ragged, and broken souls who attempted the climb.

It wouldn't matter, though, if it were Edmund Hillary attempting the climb.

It was his job to stop them.

Patrick doubled back to the entranceway into the reservoir. His destination now was the underground access to the roof of the reservoir, which opened almost invisibly from the ground, right beside the northern dome. It was painted the same white as the rest of the roof, and acted as an invisible manhole opening … like something that a spy might use.

He would pop up out of that round tunnel, and shock the hell out of the whizzers, some of whom would literally release their intended personal liquid "gift" to the community on the spot, wetting their pants instead of befouling Cleveland's water supply.

Sometimes, if he knew it was kids, he would pop up wearing a scary mask and growl. But today, at the end of his shift, dealing with a single homeless guy, he would just pop up, politely ask the man to leave, and deal with him personally if the homeless invader chose to act out.

That was his plan.

Patrick walked down the building stairwell, clean and shiny as a new car, entered the vertical accessway tunnel, and began to climb the ladder to the roof.

52

"Glad you could make it, Jack. If you don't mind my saying, you do look a bit … rough today." Cleveland's Chief of Police Calvin D. Williams had no soft spots. Zero. None. But, if he could have had one – if it were possible – he would have had a soft spot for the unlikely hero of the force … a man named Jack Wharton. One thing the chief could understand and respect is a man, or woman, willing to stand up for what they believed, and risk their life in support of those beliefs.

In Chief's eyes, Jack had shown himself to be such a man. And, that was all that mattered to the Chief. You either stood up, and made a difference, or you stayed seated, like most people do. He served the people, all the people, with respect. He just felt that most were sitters, and he had a special place for the few who stood.

That special place he now held for the fellow cop who

limped into the Cleveland City Jail and stood before him. A now-famous cop who'd come today in response to a request for help in the interrogation of the prime suspect in "the Other murders."

Interrogations are tricky. Getting someone to confess to a crime is not a simple task. Especially when the crime is capital murder.

Police interrogations haven't always been complex. Until the early 1900s, confessions obtained by "third degree" techniques were usually admissible in court as long as the suspect signed a waiver stating the confession was voluntary. These "voluntary" confessions sometimes were made after lengthy periods of deprivation of food and water, bright lights, physical discomfort, long isolation, and beatings with rubber hoses and other instruments that don't leave marks.

Modern interrogations rely instead on psychological techniques. For example, the time-honored "good cop, bad cop" routine, in which one detective browbeats the suspect and the other pretends to be looking out for them.

People tend to trust and talk to someone they perceive as their protector.

Even the physical layout of an interrogation room is designed to psychologically manipulate the suspect.

The classic interrogation manual "Criminal Interrogation and Confessions" recommends that interrogations occur in a small, soundproof room with only three chairs (two for detectives, one for the suspect), a desk, no windows, and nothing on the walls. This creates a sense of exposure, unfamiliarity, and isolation, heightening the suspect's feeling of "get me out of here".

The more stress a suspect experiences, the less likely they are to think critically and independently. This is especially true when the suspect is a minor, naïve, or mentally ill – conditions which may leave them poorly equipped to recognize or fight off manipulative tactics.

The opposite, unfortunately, is also true. For the "hard cases" – those who have become desensitized to pain from years of experiencing it, or those who have learned to play the game from years of playing it – nothing can force another human being to talk. No force on earth can force another human to say a single word if they are committed to remaining silent.

And willing to die rather than speak.

Or, perhaps more frustrating – even if another human being were forced to talk, there's no reason to believe a single word that comes out of their mouth.

Today's interrogation suspect was one of the hard cases. Since the moment one Raymond Giuseppe Antonio Cardibello was arrested, he refused to speak a single word. Not to the arresting officers, his court appointed attorney, interrogating officers. No one.

Until he went psycho and pled "Wart" in the courtroom. Then, he didn't just speak, he screamed, bellowed, and screeched until he had to be dragged out of court.

His court-appointed attorney, acting indifferently and

completely guessing, suggested his client might be expressing a willingness to perhaps talk to the man who had arrested him. The man who coincidentally grew up in the same neighborhood with him. Jack Wharton.

So, Wharton was called. And Wharton came.

"Yah. Few bumpy spots in the road, but can't complain about cushy home detail. How are things around here, Chief."

"Well, most of the National Security have left, but a few of the FBI boys are sticking around to see what happens and help out with any loose ends. But, other than that, the bad guys are still losing." The Chief didn't like to lose.

"So, I hear our suspect went a little crazy in court."

"You might say. Or you might say clever. But, he did get loud, and seemed to express an interest in maybe talking with you. You up to it?"

Jack just smiled. Once a SEAL, always a SEAL.

"They'll be bringing him from the State Pen' to the Special Interrogation room any minute. We'll let him sit in there alone with his attorney a while and then come in and see if he has anything to say. Just you and me. Coffee?"

"Whew. I thought you'd never ask."

And the two stand-up men walked and limped, side by side, to the cafeteria to enjoy a leisurely coffee.

They would both drink it black.

53

"Dee-de-lee-lee-dee-de-lee-lee, diddle lee." Like most men his age, Patrick Halloran Riley had his cell phone set with the default ring tone. It was going off now as he climbed the narrow vertical passageway up to the pop-up portal that would shortly give him access to the roof of the reservoir … where he would soon deal with his presumed would-be whizzer.

He looped one arm through the vertical ladder so he could grab his cell with the other. He was halfway to the top. He glanced at the time. Four forty-five. Fifteen minutes until the end of his shift.

"Hi honey. Just wrapping things here. What's up?"

"Just calling to see how everything's going?"

"Well, Mrs. Riley, I'll be assuming you'll be wanting an official report when I get home from church. But, since you're calling now, wife of mine who never calls, and asking in the wee hours of the morning, I'll be happy to be providing this preliminary report that all is well. I'm just about to pop up on a whizzer and shoo him off."

"Do be careful, Pat."

"Be careful? Of a whizzer? And a homeless looking shabby example of one of the precious dregs in Jesus' kingdom at that? Why, I only hope not to scare him so badly he runs off before I tell him about the food bank at the Mt. Haven Missionary, though from the looks of 'im he probably knows Cleveland resources better 'n I do."

"Still."

"You be still, woman. I'm halfway up this ladder now and if I don't get off this phone the only thing I need to be careful of is falling off. Now, don't be daft. I'll see you after church. Want me to light a candle for anything?"

"Yes, Pat. Please."

"Consider it done, woman. Now, off with you. I'm on to do my duty."

And with that, Pat hung up and continued his climb up the ladder.

It was 4:46 am.

54

Ray Cardibello and his attorney had been sitting alone in the Special Interrogation room in Cleveland's downtown jail for exactly 15 minutes. This was by design — studies have shown that 15 minutes is the peak amount of time to leave someone alone to maximize stress. Any shorter, and people left waiting experience relief. Any longer, and people left waiting start to relax. After exactly 15 minutes, Jack Wharton and Chief Calvin D. Williams walked in silently, unannounced, and sat in their chairs.

"What can you tell us about the murders of Vanessa

Altuve and the terrorist attack of the RTA?" The Chief didn't believe in messing around.

Ten seconds of silence.

"I can see we're wasting our time…" The Chief wasn't known for being patient. He began to stand, and Jack, following the Chief's lead, started to do the same.

"Well, well, well, if it isn't the 'Wart.'" Cardibello talked.

The Chief and Jack continued to stand and from a standing position, the Chief asked "You ready to talk?"

"Please, 'gentlemen'" Cardibello spat out the word, "do be seated."

Ten more seconds of silence.

The Chief and Jack sat back down.

Ten more seconds of silence.

"Well, 'Wart', how have you been?"

Jack just stared, as emotionless as the 8 on a billiard ball.

"Oh right, right, interrogation principles and all. Silence to intimidate. All right Jack, allow me to officially declare myself intimidated and permit you to move on to the next stage of this little Kabuki theater of yours." Cardibello half-smirked out of the left side of his face, which made his scar on the right side wiggle like the tail of a kite after its string had been broken.

"Let me share what I've heard, Jack," and he clanked out Wharton's name with the hardness of a jail cell closing. "I've heard you've washed out to a place where you've washed ashore, like a piece of rotten driftwood landing on the beach. I've heard...."

"Please, I must interject." The voice of Gary Stasky, Cardibello's attorney. "My client, against my counsel, has offered to provide information potentially helpful to this investigation as a courtesy, as he wishes to see justice done and the proper perpetrator of these heinous crimes apprehended. I cannot, however, allow him to make unsolicited statements which may be used in evidence in a prejudicial manner without objecting."

Stasky was a good attorney. A damn good attorney... if he wanted to be. Stasky knew both the law and the players – he was quick to cite appropriate citations and was respected by judges and prosecutors. He was tall and distinguished, an excellent speaker, and a convincing advocate.

He was a good man to have in your corner if you were in trouble...unless, of course, he believed his client had murdered a dear friend of his. If he thought that, then his client was playing a game that they couldn't win, like betting your life on the roulette wheel in Rick's Café when it's been rigged against you.

Stasky would make sure – make DAMN sure – that the minimal legalistic standards for defense would be met... and nothing more. He would make sure – make DAMN sure – that no level of appeal could successfully be made based upon incompetent defense...while at the time doing all the little things, all the tiny missteps, that would make sure – make DAMN sure – that his client didn't have a chance in HELL of being acquitted.

"Raymond Cardibello, you've been read your rights, is that correct?" it was the Chief's turn now to play the game of tie the knot on the noose.

"Oh yes, I can confirm that," Cardibello saw the game being playing clearly, and his scornful grin made it clear that he wasn't fooled, or afraid.

"And, you've heard your attorney's objection, do you still wish to continue?"

"Allow me to help this little charade move along, Chief. I have signed the document my wonderful 'counsel' has suggested I need to sign waiving my rights until such time as I reassert them. And I very, very MUCH wish to continue." His voice hissed like a coiled viper.

"Now that the legalities of this little theatrical production are over, allow me to continue. Now, where was I…."

Ten more seconds. This would be his last opportunity in a starring role and he was going to milk the spotlight.

"Ah yes. The topic at hand. What has been going on with the 'Wart' all these years…."

55

Pat H. Riley was nearly to the top of the circular, vertical access tunnel that led to the roof of the reservoir. "Daft woman" he whispered to himself. "What's she be doin' calling me at work just now? She'll go a month of Sundays not calling me once, and now here I am, trying to fit my fat arse through this damn shaft, and off goes my phone. Oww!"

During the one-sided debate he was having with himself as to the degree of slight he should feel over being interrupted by his wife at work, Pat lost his balance, slipped on the ladder a foot to the left, and his elbow banged against the wall of the narrow access tunnel.

"Mother Mary's mercy on us all." Pat's go-to saying always discharged a temper he proudly called his "Irish Ire." Patrick Halloran Riley didn't curse.

He was at the top of the tunnel now. In just a few seconds, he would pop out, shock and likely terrify one of Cleveland's lost children of the street, deliver his usual scold, threaten to have the man arrested, provide information about resources, eventually let the man go with a warning, and depending on his mood and the man's attitude, he might end up walking away with a few of Patrick Halloran Riley's freely-given hard-earned dollars in his pocket.

Just as he'd done for 27 years.

Pat grabbed the handle of the hatch, designed much like an accessway to the bridge of a submarine, and turned the large wheel that opened it. It turned easily, as the accessway, like the rest of the plant, was meticulously maintained.

"OK whizzer, if ya' whizzes ya' drawers, well, that's the Lord's own justice right there."

And…BANG!

He pushed with the force of his entire 230 pounds of former St. Ignatius Wildcat and the hatchway opened without warning. The lid banged violently and unexpectedly against the metal floor of the reservoir, sounding like a car hitting a wall without first hitting the brakes.

Pat calmly carried his significant heft through the opening and gathered himself into a standing position. He'd hoped he hadn't scared the man too badly.

"All right, all right, ya' defiler of Greater Cleveland's fine and safe drinking water! Just STOP right THERE!" Pat's command voice fit him as naturally and comfortably as the favorite sweater he wore when he petted his dog.

But, when Pat looked around, he didn't see anyone. That was unexpected. Odd, really. Usually, a homeless gent, having no clue the hatchway even existed, would be so shocked at the appearance of the big, uniformed, security officer that they'd either freeze in panic or cower into a seated position in fear.

In any case, whatever their response, they would still be there. It was only a few minutes ago that he'd seen the homeless man on the roof. Whatever athleticism these street people may have once had as youths had usually long since been eroded away by alcoholism, drugs, untreated health conditions, injuries from fights, malnutrition, and the physical deterioration from walking with a hollowed-out soul.

To have responded to the bang of the lid quickly and sprightly enough to now be outside his field of vision would require the reflexes of a real athlete … or the luck of someone who had just randomly decided to wander out of sight before the door opened.

Pat switched on his flashlight and began to look around.

"So, how should we recount the story of the 'Wart' Shall we go chronologically?" Cardibello, despite barely having a high school education, had been a well-read inmate during his various incarcerations and was no dummy.

"Let's see. Jew boy growing up in an Italian neighborhood under the beneficent protection of the other, bigger – shall I say 'braver' – other children, mostly because his parents didn't always ask for ID's to buy booze from their store.

"Kid's not just an outsider, he's a loner. A weirdo. Likes

to sit on the porch talking to himself. Smart enough to stay low and invisible. Out of the way. A weird, invisible kid in a neighborhood where Italians stood together for Italians, didn't like niggers...."

"HEY!"

The Chief did NOT like the "N word."

"...excuse me, 'African-American lads'... the same wonderful 'lads' who would abuse, harass, and rape the decent white, err... 'Caucasian' girls in the neighborhood and would have turned our own neighborhood into the kinds of slums they love to live in if we let them!"

Silence.

"So, the 'Wart' squeaks by, alternately acting the oddball or the invisible. Gets his little high school diploma, works a couple years in the Chevy plant until he starts hearing the call of military drums and decides to join the Navy. See the world! How'm I doin' so far, 'Wart'?"

And Jack looked at his tormentor of youth. He listened as this ghost of his past described the version of history that would be considered "official" – how he had been seen through the eyes of the leading psychopath of the group ... and realized that this man's recounting of events, as seen through those eyes, were THE recounting of events shared by all the boys of the neighborhood. That what he was hearing wasn't necessarily the truth, but "a" Truth, or rather, "the" consensus Truth that all the boys had seen and shared.

It was like looking at his life through a Fun House mirror

that didn't distort his physical shape, but twisted the image of his psyche into a distorted nightmare he could only barely recognize as being himself. All he could do was stare at that scar, and it seemed to him that the voice was coming from that scar, as though every word was coming out of that jagged, hideous, mocking, hellish, meandering line.

"Go on," is all he said.

57

"Come on out, ye blessed child o' the Lord scoundrel! I ain't working overtime and missin' me breakfast for the scrawny likes of a blasted buzzard whizzer man!" Pat Halloran Riley was about the only man on earth who could talk that way and still be taken seriously. "If yaz comes along peaceful, we won't be a-pressin' charges, just shoo' yaz' on ya' way! But, if I have to finds ya'! I'm liable to throw your scarecrow hide off'n this edge here."

Silence.

"All righty, then, buzzard! I'll be findin' yaz' soon enuf'. And, you won't be happy when I do now, no sir." Pat was getting a bit irked. What his friends would call "beginning to get his old Irish up." Being a good Christian man and all, he wouldn't judge the many homeless people scraping out a meager existence in the various urban mouseholes and shadow corners of the city. But, he had a job to do, and breakfast and church were waiting.

Silence still.

Most homeless people by now would have already revealed their position. Either through panic or muddy-headedness, they either would have knocked something over or tried to move and be caught in

the corners of Pat's eyes.

Nothing.

Pat began to scan the roof in the still pre-dawn dim, methodically and strategically, moving from right to left, scanning the roof with his flashlight, in a pattern not too different than if he were looking for lost keys. Did something move in the far corner, or had he heard something from behind the southern dome?

By this time, Pat was not in a mood for any more charmingly-Irish, friendly warnings, and silently crept around the dome to the point where he thought he'd heard something. Keeping his back to the dome and shuffling along like someone walking along the ledge of a building high above the ground, Pat poured himself around the edge surprisingly smoothly for a man of his age and bulk.

He heard the sound again. From the same spot. Just a wee bit further around the corner....

By now, his heart surprised him by racing along. Why would a homeless whizzer give him the willies? But, he'd long since learned to trust his instincts, and something didn't feel quite right. So, he continued to carry himself smoothly, stealthily, and under control.

He took a deep, silent breath…and continued on.

A few more feet…another step…another…just about there…

SNAP!

…his foot broke a random twig underfoot making a sharp sound!

"SQUEAK!"

"Squeak, squeak, squeak, squeak. SQUEAK!"

"Oh, for the love of…"

A rat.

A four-legged member of "God's creatures", caught in one of the traps planted about the grounds to knock down the pest problem, squealed in panic to escape! There it (do people think of rats in traps as "he" or "she") was hopelessly stuck in a kind of flypaper that held "it" in final fatal embrace – "its" every effort to break free only entangling it more torturously.

"Funny, I don't remember 'em laying any of these blasted traps on the roof up here," he muttered to himself. Pat straightened up, wiped his brow, and scratched his big Irish head.

Pat didn't believe in letting animals suffer, so he looked around and, seeing a random brick by the other dome, walked over to pick it up as a tool to end this poor creature's suffering.

He whistled a bit of "When Irish Eyes are Smiling". He bent over to pick up the brick…

…and felt someone jump him from behind and put their arm under his chin so he couldn't breathe.

58

"Sure thing, Wart. I'll go on.

"So, our new war hero decides to go all in. He's not just going to be a regular Navy boy circle-jerking his fellow sailors below deck. No, he's going to become a big, bad Navy SEAL.

"And, lo and behold, somehow, by the skin of his Jewish dick, he makes it. Our hero – the Jew boy from Murray Hill, is now a big, bad Navy SEAL. Hit the big time. 'Course, his folks aren't around anymore to see it, but there he is – with the fancy hat and tattoo and every-thing – all ready to go off and fight the terrorists for the red, white, and blue."

Jack could hardly stand listening to his harsh, hypnotic voice, seemingly speaking from that long angry gash that stretched from Cardibello's mouth to his ear. He felt like he was sinking into it, falling, disconnecting from his ego and self-identity, drifting away….

"Let me tell you something." The Chief's voice was a whisper every bit as menacing as the hiss from a volcanic fissure that might erupt any moment. "The man you are speaking of and to is 'Inspector Jack Wharton' to you."

Cardibello stiffened briefly, and then, slowly responded with a grin that had been asymmetric for a long, long time. "Very well, Chief", he sounded almost cheerful. "The honorable 'Inspector Jack Wharton' then. Indeed and of course.

"So, the right honorable now Inspector was then a Navy SEAL. Only something happens. No one knows what, exactly. Rumor has it it's the booze, but lots of sailors drink, now, don't they? Very few of them get washed out for it. So, what was the reason Inspector Jack Wharton ends up getting an administrative discharge? Care to fill us in, Jack?"

"We're here to talk about a series of murders you committed, maggot." The Chief wasn't known, of course, for patience. "Do you have something to add, or don't you? Counselor, please advise your client that interrogations are admissible as evidence and providing false leads during an investigation can be seen by a jury as evidence of culpability." The Chief wasn't just a hard-ass. He also knew the law.

"Mr. Cardibello", Gary Stasky, Esquire intoned, some-how managing not to sound completely bored. "Inter-rogations are admissible as evidence and providing false leads during an investigation can be seen by a jury as evidence of culpability." By the book. The minimum amount of legal direction possible to avoid potential grounds for overturning the inevitable conviction.

"Hahahahahahaha!" Cardibello burst into a laugh so

hearty one would have thought it was from Ebenezer Scrooge on Christmas morn' after his visitations from the three ghosts!

59

It had been a long time – a long time – since Pat Halloran Riley had been on the wrestling team at St. Ignatius. It had been an equally long time since he played center on the football team. It had been almost as long since Pat Halloran Riley had seriously trained or worked out.

But, the big Irishman hadn't forgotten how to fight.

Most people, when choked from behind, will instinctively pull forward, tightening the grip of their assailant. Pat, however, did exactly the opposite. He hunched his shoulders, leaned backward as far as he could, and began to backpeddle. Although he was attacked from behind, he did have one advantage. He outweighed his assailant by a good 20 pounds.

The two careened backward in odd embrace, like two people dancing an awkward, clumsy, bizarre tango, or a dog riding a bear. But Pat knew eventually, eventually, if he could just hold on, the dancing pair would come across something – some object that would interrupt their macabre waltz.

And they did. About 10 feet from the point of the assault was a foot-high brick ledge. It never seemed to serve any purpose. It was just some random low fence, as though

the contractors added random structures and outcrop-
pings to be able to charge for additional bricklayers'
time laying bricks.

And it was right in the path of the retreating duo. Just
as Pat was about to see spots, the two backed into that
random brick wall, and they both toppled backward
over it – Pat falling with his substantial girth on top of
his assailant.

"Oooof!"

The big Irishman's weight broke his assailant's grip.

Pat was winded, but knew that, when a fighter's got his
man down, he's got to pounce. And pounce he did. Only
in his anger, he didn't think to continue to use his weight
advantage and instead lashed out with both fists. Like
any good Irishman would, he was set on blackening his
opponent's eyes, breaking his nose, and sending him into
dreamland with his ham fists.

WHACK! WHACK! WHACK!

Pat immediately knew that this was a very odd sound,
but once he got his "Irish" up, there was no stopping,
so he continued to punch his opponent, even as the
punches didn't resonate with the sound of fist on flesh
at all. And, his fists started taking an awful beating themselves while his homeless-looking opponent continued to
rise to his feet, even while absorbing the big man's blows.

"He's wearing pads!" Pat Halloran Riley had played
center on the football team and knew what it felt like
to punch the plastic armor football players wear. In his

anger, and with his time on the gridiron being so long ago, it took him longer to figure out he was punching padding than it would have taken in his youth.

And, that delay led to a tragic result.

Because, now he could see his assailant was wearing a mesh mask, with some sort of hard plastic layer underneath. Pat stopped punching and froze in confusion for just a moment – staring at the bizarre, armored, home-less-looking man in front of him…

…a metallic flash in the dawning sun…

…zwipp!

…and, he heard the sound of material tearing and felt a pain stretching across his entire abdomen.

"Hahahahahaha!" Cardibello sounded like the guy every stand-up comedian would love to have sitting in the front row.

"Evidence against me? Evidence AGAINST me?!?" He was almost out of breath from laughing, panting out the words like someone who was repeating lines from the funniest joke they'd ever heard. "What in the hell for? Ahahaha! We both know – we ALL know – that there won't be any need for any evidence against me! That's not how this story ends! Stop telling bad jokes, OFFI-CERS! You've got the wrong punch line!"

His two beefy, bookend, African-American escorts from the penitentiary had already quickly burst into the room and were ready to control their charge, if need be.

"No! No need, gentlemen! I'm not about to attack nobody! Please, allow me to enjoy this wonderful joke first presented by the Chief and then echoed, oh so helpfully, for the record by my esteemed counselor.

"Allow me to rejoinder. We both know none of this has anything to do with me. We all know there will never be any need for 'evidence.' I didn't come here to give you any information you don't already know. I came to make you face what you already DO know!

"Because, YOU did this! All of YOU! It's you who helped create the fear of the other. Every time you jack up some Mexican kid on the street because he's Mexican. Maybe, he's an illegal, or if not, why not say he's a gang member. 'You got a receipt for that hat, kid? No? Too bad.'

"Meanwhile, the white kid selling drugs around the corner you just happen not to see…cuz his dad works for the mayor! YOU did this! Every time you shoot some Black guy because YOU can't tell the difference between a gun and a cell phone … if some poor Black dude happens to be holding it!

"You want to know why people fear the other? Because YOU need them to! You ARE the other! You KNOW that's true!!"

The Chief nodded to Mr. Cardibello's chaperones.

"WAIT! You wanted to hear what I have to say!" Cardibello's rant time was coming to an end as his chaperones had already grabbed his elbows. His performance was about to be booed off the stage.

"Just this! You want to know about these murders! Look in the mirror! LOOK IN THE MOTHERFUCKING MIRROR! Wart! Wart! Waaaaaaaaaaaaaarrrrrrr-rtttttt!!!!!" And, with that, he was dragged out and off, leaving a diminishing screech as he was carted off – a screech that sounded like a lonely train whistle drifting into the distance, or the melting Wicked Witch of West fading away.

Gary Stasky calmly closed his laptop, put it and his legal pad into his case, nodded to Jack and the Chief with only the slightest, imperceptible grin, and walked out.

"Well, that was a fucking waste of time."

That was the first and only time Jack Wharton heard the Chief swear.

61

Pat Halloran Riley had been in his share of rucks. Had even been stuck a time or two. But, he'd never been stabbed like this. So expertly. So devastatingly. So finally.

But, he was still one Irishman not going down without a fight, and he'd learned a few things playing the Black teams on the football field back in the day. A few "special moves." Moves that weren't exactly according to the rules. Moves that, if they were made against your team, an honest Irish lad might call "dirty."

For one, there are places in a man's body that can't be padded or else they can't move. Behind the joints, for example. Like…behind the KNEE!

And Pat, using a move he'd learned long ago on a football field, spun his right foot around and behind his murderer and drove it into the back of his left knee.

"Uhhhhnnnn!"

His opponent was briefly stunned and dropped a bag of something he'd been carrying …

…but regained his composure and gave the knife another turn.

Even though he knew he was dying, Pat felt good about that blow. But already his strength was waning too quickly for him to follow up. He still remembered, though, how to get under someone's pads, and with his remaining strength, he thrust his powerful, large hand beneath the facial shield of his opponent and grabbed. His hand came away with some remnant of that shield with a snap…and the big Irishman slumped to the ground.

And began to fade away.

The world, for Pat, began to dim and shrink. He thought of his wife. He thought of her on that trip they'd planned to Hawaii, a trip she would insist on taking alone for his sake and in his memory. She thought of her meeting a nice man about her age on that trip. Someone who, while she would never be intimate with, was a widower himself…and the two of them would provide comfort and companionship together – a rare and beautiful friendship that allowed the two of them to share memories of their dearly departed for years and years…keeping those precious memories alive for the rest of their time on earth.

Pat's world darkened even more, and he became frightened, but only for an instant. Because, he saw an old familiar face in an old familiar place. He saw the face of the grey-haired, kindly Father Jim McAllister, the dearly-departed Pastor of St. Ignatius when he was just a freshman Wildcat, new to the school.

And, Father McAllister came down from the altar where he had been performing mass the way Pat was first taught – in Latin, with the priest facing the altar, his back to the congregation.

"In nomine Patris, et Filii, et Spiritus Sancti" Pat could hear the priest's powerful, sonorous voice.

"Amen," Pat answered the Father, who turned around to Pat, smiled and, giving him Communion, said "I knew me Patrick would always find his way back to church."

As they left the interrogation room, the Chief took Jack by the arm.

"You okay?"

Brief hesitation.

"Yah, I'm fine."

The Chief looked at Jack for an expectant second. In the eyes. Like he was confused at something he'd just seen and was peering in for some explanation.

"Like you said, Chief. Fucking waste of time."

With that Jack hobbled out, the Chief watching him for a full two seconds before getting on with his day.

The homeless-looking man atop the Garrett A. Morgan Water Treatment Plant had seen his plans ruined by a lummox security guard. Instead of having already poured the contents of his bag into the city of Cleveland's drinking water and taken off, he had scattered much of his precious weapon onto the rooftop and the rest of the bag, now torn, was too dangerous to handle in its current state.

His clothing, as it was designed, would protect him

from skin absorption, but his filtered mask had gotten damaged in the aggravating brawl. Even now, he couldn't be sure that some of the chemical agent he'd brought hadn't already found its way into his lungs, which lent an urgency to his departure.

And, with his damaged leg – thanks to this imbecilic rent-a-cop – he wasn't sure he could properly scale the dome to get to the opening to deliver his toxin anyway.

Down below, a car pulled into the lot – headlights sweeping across the front of the building. The driver would be the relief shift for the late Pat Halloran Riley in the form of Dave Dzedzedski, right on time as usual.

The homeless-looking man made his way to the exact same tunnel that the man he'd killed used to surprise him. He'd been trained to be resourceful in the face of unexpected circumstances, but he knew that this mission had failed, thwarted by a man who had given his life to protect water.

The homeless-looking man closed the hatch and went down the ladder.

He would exit the grounds as he had entered it – carefully, silently, stealthily – as he'd been trained to do. Sometimes crawling, sometimes scurrying from cover to cover. Through the woods. Through the hole in the fence. To his car. And home.

It would be nearly an hour before the body of Patrick Halloran Riley, a man who would be remembered as a hero, would be found. Still clutching the strap he'd pulled from his murderer's mask.

Beside him, scrawled in red on the ground.

Three words.

"That is all."

"LSD?!? Are you sure?!" Cleveland's Chief of Police had been through a lot recently and this latest news was doing his head completely in. "What would a drug dealer be doing on the roof of the reservoir with a bag full of LSD? And, why would Riley be up there tangling with him to get himself killed?

"Could Riley have been …'involved'?" The Chief always had a hard time accepting that there were "dirty cops" on his force, and had a difficult time even finding the right words.

"Oh yes, Chief, no doubt about it. Perhaps as much as a quarter kilo in powder form." Neil Kendricks-Johnson, aka "The Professor" was presenting his incredible report as best he could. Even at that, he knew he was "burying the lede" in the story, but the BIG news would have to wait a few moments for another professional, soon to join them, to make. For now, his duty was to report on the specific forensic evidence and his interpretation of events.

"But, we don't believe Riley was…'involved.'"

"Ok then, let me get this straight, KJ. Someone, or

'someones', brings a quarter kilo of LSD in a bag up to the roof of the Garrett A. Morgan reservoir. There, he meets, or encounters, a Security Officer, weeks from retirement who served for 27 years without the slightest mark on his record. Somehow, the two of them get into some kind of fight, and this person, or persons, stabs our man to death, drops the bag, and leaves. Is that what you're telling me happened?"

"Basically, that's true, Chief, but there is more…"

"Hold on. Before we go further. You're saying a quarter kilo. Maybe half a pound. A quarter kilo of LSD. Do you know the value of that? It has to be over ten million dollars worth of LSD, left scattered atop the damn reservoir!"

"More like 25 million dollars worth, sir."

The Chief stroked his chin to keep his head from exploding.

"Twenty five million dollars worth…well, cops have turned bad for less…."

"There is more sir. We don't think this is a drug deal gone bad. Look at this picture."

The Chief looked at the picture of the three words the homeless-looking assassin had left scrawled atop the reservoir roof.

"'That is all'?" The Chief's instincts had been honed from years of having to be the baddest cat in the urban jungle, and right now, those instincts were screaming at him. Nonetheless, he was a trained cop, and had to methodically eliminate each possibility.

"That's the horse hockey that psycho 'Other' used as his calling card. Could we have a copy-cat? The 'That is all' hot air was in all the papers." The Chief knew he was grasping at straws, but the idea that they had the wrong man in jail – that this psychotic terrorist was still on the loose – was something he was hoping against hope wasn't true…even though his instincts had no doubt that this was the case.

"Doubtful. We've had handwriting look at it, and there are some similarities. In addition, it's forensics' opinion that a copycat would be unlikely to use the errr…the err, partial remains to write the words." This was as delicately as Kendricks-Johnson could say that it was unlikely a copycat would use his victim's blood to write the words and use the victim's hand as his writing tool.

A knock on the door, and in walked the professional they'd be awaiting – FBI Agent Thomas Gibson, one of the members of the Just Another investigative team originally assembled to capture The Other.

"We don't need our garbage cans cleaned." The Chief could show a sense of humor, when he wanted, and had a long memory. He also didn't like when people made assumptions about the women and men under his command.

Agent Gibson calmly walked over to the trash can, picked it up and left. He came back in 30 seconds with an empty waste basket. In fact, he'd emptied every single waste basket in the office.

No word of the prior incident was ever spoken again.

"How's the family, Chief?" Agent Gibson was a Southern boy at heart, and believed in being polite. Was raised to let people know he cared.

"The Mrs. had to go in for her back again, but the kids are doing well. DeShone got admitted to Case."

There's was more than a little pride in the Chief's voice with that one. Cleveland's exclusive Case Western Reserve University had an acceptance rate of only 35% and was rated the number 37 university in the country by US News and World Report.

"Lot to be proud of right there, Chief. Lot to be proud of. Your son must work awfully hard. Guess'n he might have got some of that from his dad?" Agent Gibson had more than a touch of Southern charm, as well.

If the Chief could blush, he might have, but he briskly played it off. "The one thing he learned from me is that if you don't get good grades, you might end up being a cop."

The ice properly broken, Agent Gibson began his report.

"I imagine Mr. Kendricks-Johnson…"

"Please, call me KJ". Kendricks-Johnson was a head taller than the FBI man and at least 50 pounds heavier. Polite or not, the agent wasn't about to refer to the big forensics specialist by any term other than the term he'd been asked. Of course, the request was obviously intended to express warm regards and more importantly, respect. That message crosses all cultures.

"Thank you." The agent nodded and resumed.

"I'm sure … KJ has brought you up to speed regarding the contents of the bag we've found on the roof of the Garrett A. Morgan Water Treatment Plant?"

"Over 25 million dollars' worth of LSD."

"Exactly. And the writing on the floor of the building."

"That same psychotic nonsense as before. Doesn't prove anything." The Chief's mind was still fighting a battle with his instincts he knew he was going to lose, but was playing his hand out as he'd been trained – to consider every possibility.

"You are correct, sir. No, it does not. But, I do have something from some security film that you need to see," and Agent Gibson took several photographs out of an envelope he'd been carrying. "You gentlemen will see here in this photograph a blowup of a picture taken of the perpetrator who attacked the RTA rail car."

"I recall that none of those pictures were of any use to us whatsoever." The Chief kept playing cards he already knew were about to be trumped.

"You are, of course, quite correct again, sir. At least so far as the utility of those images in helping us identify the face of the culprit. As we discussed earlier, through some means we have yet to understand, he was able to strategically turn his face throughout the monitored area in such a way as to have either his hat, or his hand, or some other object blocking the camera.

"However, I do bring to your attention a particular article of clothing here, that the cameras did capture, sir. I speak specifically of his hat."

"Ok, he's wearing a hat." The Chief knew he should already have tossed in his hand and folded, but wasn't ready to accept the horrible reality until the last card was played out.

"We do have some long distance footage of some of the battle between Officer Riley and his assailant from a live stream television weather camera. We've blown it up and enhanced it as best we can and are still trying to interpret the images we see from the assailant's face. But, there is something from this picture here the FBI believes is compelling evidence."

And, the Chief looked at the blown-up, enhanced-though-still-pixelated photograph of the person who murdered Security Officer Patrick Halloran Riley. The Chief was observant by nature, and those skills were sharpened like razors from training and experience. He immediately saw the card that won the pot – the pot he wanted not to lose more than money.

"The same hat." The Chief gave voice to the conclusive card. The terrorist who bombed the RTA rail car and the man who murdered Officer Riley were wearing the exact same hat. A red MAGA hat with a distinctive, customized, extended brim.

"Re-organize the investigative team," the Chief ordered as though he were commanding a star ship into warp drive. "And, get me that lawyer, Stasky. I want to talk to his client again, only this time, I won't be so nice."

"So, how does it feel to be fired from being a hero?" Johnson was, as always, creatively poetic in his applying salt to the wound, but he knew softer-sounding words would only make his partner feel worse.

Johnson had long understood that it was his job to help Jack get through the dark times when he would question his worth as a human being. It was what Johnson was created for.

The headlines atop the Cleveland Plain Dealer splayed out on the Batcave coffee table read "DID 'HERO COP' NAB THE WRONG MAN? Calls for Calm as 'The Other' Investigative Team Reconvenes."

"Well, pard'ner, hero wasn't a job I ever really wanted."

Jack was in a dark place – his body beaten and battered from his battle with the wrong man, and now with an equally battered ego to match. Not only had he had his soul slowly filleted by his ex-wife, but the entire world – the same "world" that had just been parading him around like Captain America – saw him now as a glory-seeking fraud. A masquerading imposter. A Western sheriff turned bad.

"Fair enough, Jack." Even Johnson couldn't use his usual nickname of "Wart" today. "And, truth be told, you did do me a huge favor by leaving my name out of it, which I appreciate. No point in both of us going down. Someone has to be available to still fight for truth, justice, and the American way."

"All that work. The probability charts! How many case studies did we consider, compile, collate, dissect, statistically arrange into probability models? Right here in these rooms!

"And, it was working! Your model – yes, it was YOURS – that model correctly predicted the likelihood of Cardibello using a bus to escape – you damn near predicted the exact date!

"That's the heroic policework. That's long days and nights poring over reports, researching and interpreting data, looking at every nuance, every category of likely human behavior. Calculating every potential move, every conceivable option from every conceivable angle until a picture became visible through a digital crystal ball, like that Oz bitch – what's her name – 'Auntie 'Em'.

"All I did was act on a hunch. A guess. Something I think I just dreamed up."

The two both took long simultaneous pulls off their beers – gold can Coors, not Coors Lites.

"Fuck Auntie 'Em."

"Look, we both know you don't always put fires out with water. Sometimes, you've got to use gasoline! Fight fire with fire. To catch this psycho who masqueraded as a homeless person, I figured I'd impersonate a homeless person myself."

"Dude, you pulled that off great! You nearly got jumped by the crowd thinking some homeless nut was mugging a guy in the Greyhound!" Johnson, deep down, was supportive of his lifelong partner, despite his reflexive insults.

"For what? For WHAT?!? A few rolls in the hay with my ex only to later have her tell me she hated every second? Maybe, a wrongful arrest suit, if not an indictment for assault? Being put on a national pedestal for a couple weeks only to have it all turn into a nightmare? To have my name become a bad joke? How did this become my life? All I did was try to be a good cop!"

The two took simultaneous pulls off their beers, like mirror images, as though cued by a buzzer.

"Do you know what's trending on Twitter right now? #wrongguy What the hell is wrong with people?"

"People are fucked."

"To protect and serve. Isn't that our motto?"

A third mirror-image dual pull off their beers.

"So, now what, Jack? The old team getting back together?"

"That's the plan. Only this time, they're adding some new hot shot. Some Washington broad."

"I'm sure that has this psycho asshole ready to just turn himself in. Any chance it could still be Cardibello?"

No answer. None needed.

A final encore of the two mirroring each other's beer drinking, ending in simultaneous emptying.

Jack took both cans to the kitchen and opened the fridge.

He didn't have to ask if his partner was ready for another.

A prison is a jungle inside a jungle – highly organized, structured, intricate as a spider web – interwoven with rival encampments of army ant people pledged to obey the orders of their group, their clan, their gang…

…their family.

A prison jungle is different than the type of urban jungle one might find in a downtown Greyhound station at night – different in the way that touch football is different from the way Aztecs played soccer.

A prison jungle is comprised of the most violent people, mostly men, on earth.

A sophisticated, Darwinian subculture based on loyalty, security, and respect – whose rules are enforced by one consequence for those who break them.

The same consequence that befell the losing team in ancient Aztec soccer.

That means of enforcement certainly applied to the jungle in the maximum security ward boweled deep within the Ohio State Penitentiary. Now home for a certain famous suspect. A certain suspect with a very distinctive scar.

Ray Cardibello wasn't a highly-educated man, but he had a PhD from the "Hard Knocks U" when it came to the jungle inside a prison. This deep understanding, combined with a street panther's instincts, were how he'd managed to survive his previous incarcerations.

Cardibello was both a prisoner in this jungle and a senior member of it. He knew the rules, believed in them, and had personally enforced them…more than once.

He had believed he'd seen, from the beginning, how his future within this primordial world was going to play out. At this point, he was neither afraid nor angry.

A bit reflective, but he could see clearly. The future. The past. The present.

Like a Buddhist monk. He simply accepted the script about to be played out, already knowing the ending with perfect certainty … like watching a movie based on a book he'd already read.

As indifferent as a leaf upon a stream.

Mostly, he was just curious about a few details. That was all.

He heard a click behind him. He didn't move or even look.

"If I'd known you were coming," he said, "I'd have baked a cake."

67

"So, who's the new spook heading our team? Anyone know anything about her?" Chief Buddy O' Malley, of the Ohio State Highway Patrol, was a good cop. While he wasn't always considered the sharpest tool in the shed, he was generally respected for his diligence, integrity, and willingness to talk straight. While that could sometimes get him in trouble, he was a good cop. No one ever questioned that.

He asked his question, an unaimed arrow, to the collection of investigators in the room, but it fell without striking a single individual target. The others in the room, unlike the Highway Patrol Officer, had filters that prevented them from voicing thoughts that might cast them in a negative professional light.

"I mean, I Googled 'Carla Brandon', but only came up with one official bio paragraph of blah, blah, blah. Not a single reference in a news article. Not even a LinkedIn or Facebook. It's like she's Internet invisible. Anyone hear anything? What's a Carla Brandon?"

The original investigation team, once called "Just Another" but this time with no nickname, were in the room. Amongst those in attendance who had ducked the patrolman's verbal arrow were: FBI video specialist Agent Sjoltsen Vinjrud; FBI Agent Thomas Gibson, he who had graduated top of his class;

Cleveland's local forensics genius, "the Professor" Neil

Kendricks-Johnson; Tina Blair Johnston, of the National Security Agency, whose reports were thorough but who never spoke; the team's former head, Cleveland's Chief of Police, Calvin D. Williams; a handful of nondescript paper-pushers with outstanding credentials; and, of course, the now-fallen hero Jack Wharton.

Someone coughed and the door to the meeting room opened.

And, it was Gillian Anderson's clone. Short, bright red hair pulled back, pert figure, pouty lips with red lipstick, intelligent eyes, wearing low heels, a power pants suit, button down blouse, a snappy vest, and with a determined stride and erect posture … Dana Scully walked into the room.

"The truth is out there…" came an anonymous whisper.

Scully's doppelganger said nothing. She calmly opened her thin black attaché and removed a black folder marked "Letters of Authorization". From this folder, she removed several other, plain-looking, full-sized, 8 ½ by 11 inch envelopes.

"Lady and gentlemen", she correctly began as there was only one other female, other than herself, in the room. Her voice came from the abdomen, like an opera singer's voice, and effortlessly filled the room.

"It will be helpful for everyone to understand what I have in my hands. These envelopes contain authorization of authority letters from each of your respective organizations, departments, and government agencies. They are all signed by the respective agency and organization heads, including the heads of the National Security Agency, the Federal Bureau of Investigation, the Governor of Ohio, and the Mayor of Cleveland.

"Each and every one of these letters proffer upon myself the absolute authority to act in these respective organizational leaders' stead. I am entirely empowered to direct each and every one of you to perform tasks to whatever specifications and standards I choose. I am fully empowered to enact whatever consequences I choose should those tasks not be carried out to my complete and entire satisfaction.

"Beyond this, I have, thoughtfully I would think, obtained authorization from the Pentagon to amend the status of those of you who have military backgrounds. I can, without need for any additional authorization or signature, convert inactive retired status to emergency active status and involuntarily re-enlist you. That is to say, in effect, if you've ever served in the military before, I can have you 'drafted'. Today. Now.

"I am further empowered to terminate the employment of each and every one of you and do so in a way that removes any pensions, retirement benefits, or other post-employment entitlements.

"If you make official request to personally read the respective letter of authorization pertaining to your circumstances, I will gladly provide access to it. Of course, that's only potential. You have no way of knowing how willing and capable I am to exercise my authority. Anyone wishing to obtain that information need only give me a reason to demonstrate. I will gladly and effectively do so.

"Let me provide further clarification. I've been reading the reports previously generated by this investigative group and I am … unimpressed."

The way she said "unimpressed" felt like a profanity. A really bad profanity.

"You've flailed about like you were trained by Barney Fife, and based upon what I've read, I wouldn't trust any one of you with his single bullet. That's going to change."

Agent Brandon put the envelopes containing the letters of authorization, which no one asked to see, back into the leather folder, and put that folder back into her case. She pulled several other folders out of her case like someone performing an autopsy might remove suspect organs. She took 10 seconds doing so, which barely gave the group in attendance time to relax their sphincters.

"Today, we're going to get organized. There are several specific areas of investigative focus that we are going to find answers to. Firstly, I expect a report today on the LSD left behind in the murder of the reservoir security officer. I have asked two of you, FBI Agent Gibson and Cleveland's Lead Forensics Officer, Neil Kendricks-Johnson, to provide a briefing on that chemical agent.

"I've been particularly … unimpressed", and that word, again, chafed like a t-shirt against a marathon runner's nipple, "unimpressed" she repeated, "by your inability and ultimate ignoring of the unanswered video conundrum surrounding the Rapid Transit terrorist attack. It's one thing to leave unanswered the question of who would even know where the cameras are, but lady and gentleman, the terrorist didn't just vanish. We are going to find out where he went and why his departure wasn't captured on any surveillance cameras. We will be establishing, today, a video team who will be personally responsible, not professionally responsible, for finding that answer.

"We will further create a team to investigate the evidence found in the hand of the slain reservoir officer, a piece of what appears to be an elastic strap. I've asked Kendricks-Johnson and Gibson to provide a preliminary report on that today, as well.

"The final investigation focus team we will form today will be to fully obtain whatever information this Ray Cardibello might possess. While it's apparent he's not the murderer we seek, my reading of what he has already said lead me to believe he has information potentially helpful to this investigation. We will obtain this information through any means necessary, including the granting of limited immunity…or other creative, interrogative methods. I have the authority to use harsh methods here, as well.

"These will be the four immediate, priority, areas of investigative focus we will be forming teams to find answers regarding. If you value your … current situations, you will be finding those answers.

"And, before we go further. One final thought.

"If any one of you. Ever. Make a single X-Files refer-ence..." her voice was very quiet now.

"I. Will. Personally. Fuck. You. Up."

For the first time anyone could remember, Tina Blair Johnston, of the National Security Agency, the quiet one in the group, smiled. Her smile was an outlier, as the rest of the team were as stone-faced as the statues on Easter Island.

"Now, Kendricks-Johnson and Gibson. Your report on the LSD discovered on the scene of murder at the Garrett A. Morgan Water Treatment Plant, if you please. The floor is yours."

"Th…, thank you, Agent Brandon" FBI agent Gibson began, halting only a moment before finding his legs.

"Before moving to the specifics of the LSD and its possi-ble origin (which will be discussed in depth shortly), Officer Kendricks-Johnson and I would like to go over, for the rest of the team, the report describing the oper-ational theory as to the chronology of the murder of Chief Security Inspector Riley."

"Please proceed." With two words, Agent Brandon sent the message that, when she asked for something, that "something" was what she expected to receive, but that she also respected the reasonable judgment of the team she was newly in firm charge of.

"It appears that sometime around 4:30 am, Inspector Riley had some reason to believe there was an intruder. We've tracked his footsteps to the eastern slope of the property and into a wooded area. We have ascertained that this wooded area is a place where homeless people occasionally cut through the fence to sleep.

"Since Inspector Riley's normal rounds did not typically include going into that area a half hour before his shift was to end, we believe he saw or heard something suspicious. We also found footprints of what appear to be military-style boots worn by a presumed intruder, whom we believe committed the murder.

"It should be noted that Inspector Riley was a highly experienced officer, and it was his experience that intruders would sometimes go atop the reservoir to… attempt to contaminate the water as a prank."

"Whizzers!" Patrolman O' Malley chimed in and immediately regretted it.

"Patrolman O' Malley, isn't it?" Agent Brandon had done her homework before the meeting and had obviously learned to identify the members of her team from pictures.

"Yes, Agent Brandon. Chief Highway Patrolman Beauregard O' Malley, at your service, ma'am! But, everyone calls me 'Buddy.'"

It was impossible to tell if his attempts at Irish charm

were working or if their new team leader was simply tolerating him, but Agent Brandon calmly asked "Can you please elaborate on what a 'whizzer' is?"

"Whizzers," O' Malley answered, "were the colloquial name given by Inspector Riley to a collective group of periodic vandals who, as has been suggested, would attempt to contaminate the water supply. The reason he referred to them as 'whizzers' is because the method chosen to perform this contamination was to…p'… urinate into the water from the air openings atop the twin geodesic domes on the reservoir roof."

No one had ever heard O' Malley speak so eloquently. Neither had anyone ever heard that "Buddy" O' Malley's real name was Beauregard.

"The relatively minuscule amount of urine from a human being deposited into such a vast body of water does not significantly affect the water quality, but if people became aware of the practice, it might undermine the public's confidence in the safety of their drinking water.

"Inspector Riley took the protection of our drinking water as something of a sacred calling, ma'am. He took it seriously. He also had concern that someone might injure themselves from climbing the dome, as it's not an easy thing to do.

"Mostly, it'd be stoned out kids from Cleveland State performing some hazing ritual or prank, or occasionally some homeless person would try it as an act of delirious rebellion against a society that they felt was p'… urinating on them, but Inspector Riley would usually catch 'em before they could complete their mission. Usually catch 'em all."

The group was rapt at the Highway Patrolman's insights. Truth be told, he told a pretty fair story.

"There was an emergency access portal coming up onto the roof that opened from a hatch that was barely visible. He liked to pop that old hatch open, and just read the 'whizzers' the riot act! Inspector Riley was a big man – a St. Ignatius Wildcat, don't you know – and he'd put the fear of God in 'em good!

"For the college kids, he'd make a deal out of marching them to the office and taking their names. Then, he'd let 'em go with a warning. Ten minutes later, he'd throw their names in the waste basket with a laugh! Not one of those kids would ever come back!

"For the random homeless guy, he'd first put the fear of God in 'em, and then see what he could do to help them with a saint's grace."

Five second pause.

"Anyway, Agent Brandon, that's what a 'whizzer' is?"

"I'm impressed, Agent… 'Buddy'," Agent Brandon began, "may I ask how you know all this?"

Five second pause.

"You see ma'am…well, you know us Irishmen….'Wildcat Riley' and I used to enjoy a few pints of Guinness from time to time together, we surely did."

The Highway Patrolman had something in his eye.

"I would like to catch his murderer, Agent Brandon, I surely would."

Agent Brandon, she with the Letters of Authorization of Authorities in her case, calmly pushed herself from the table, stood up, walked over to the place where the Highway Patrolman was sitting, stood behind him, put her right hand on his right shoulder with a firm grip, held her head high like she was saying the Pledge of Allegiance, and said simply, "I do too, mister. I do too."

She then, just as calmly, walked back to her seat.

"Agent Gibson," she said, "Please continue your report."

"Thank you," Agent Gibson continued. "As so color-fully described by Buddy here, our evidence indicates Inspector Riley apparently confronted his assailant on the roof and a fight ensued.

"I would like to direct your attention now to the follow-ing photographs" and a projector turned on.

"What you are looking at are the framework bars for the geodesic dome atop the reservoir, magnified 200 times. These bars are what 'whizzers', err... climbers use as ladder rungs to get to the top of the dome. You'll note tiny black fibers on images one through four, and no such fibers on images five through eight.

"We believe these fibers are from gloves used by the person who murdered Inspector Riley. This is significant – the images from the framework bars one through four are from the lower portion of the geodesic dome. The images from the bars five through eight are from the upper portion of the dome."

"So, he never reached the top," Buddy O' Malley murmured loud enough to hear. "The Wildcat usually stopped 'em, usually stopped 'em every time."

"That is our interpretation of the evidence as well, Patrolman. We believe that Inspector Riley interrupted the attempt to poison our water supply and prevented this terrorist from committing his terrorist attack."

"I will make a point of releasing this information to the press, after the family is first notified, of course" Agent Brandon announced. "It will be recorded that Inspector Riley did not die in vain. Please continue."

"The following images are from a distant, rotating television camera located atop the Terminal Tower downtown. As the camera rotates, the relevant images capture only portions of the battle, and the distance and age of the equipment make the imagery very pixelated and blurry.

"Several important conclusions can, nonetheless, be drawn from these images. One, as I'm sure you've all read in the pre-meeting report, the hat worn by this would-be terrorist is virtually identical to the hat worn by the terrorist responsible for the Rapid Transit massacre. Meaning, he almost certainly is the same man.

"The second conclusion was reached from examining the next two images. You'll see if you look carefully, in image one B, that Inspector Riley has delivered what appears to be an upper-cut into the mid-section of his assailant. In image two B, taken one second later, the assailant's body and clothing do not appear to have been affected at all by this blow.

"We found this peculiar, as Inspector Riley was not a small man and was known, in his younger days, for having been involved in periodic aggressive interactions."

"Oh, the Wildcat always enjoyed a good ruck, that's for sure! He and I had a few kerfuffles ourselves! I'd like to see the man who could stand there and take his uppercut like that and just laugh 'er off, I can tell you!" Buddy was enjoying the reminisce, and felt some better to know his fallen friend would be remembered as having died a hero.

"So would we, Patrolman," Agent Gibson continued. "We've been examining other evidence on the scene and have a working theory that this assailant was wearing some type of body armor under his clothing, like a motorcyclist or athlete might wear, modified for combat."

"Then it weren't a fair fight!" O' Malley was angry now. "I knew it!!" and the Patrolman slammed the table and wept quietly. The others in the room made him instantly invisible to them, out of respect, and silently committed to amnesia, as well.

"In addition to these photos and conclusions derived therefrom," Gibson continued, "we also have three pieces of valuable evidence from the scene to discuss. The first are the words, 'That is All', now widely known to be associated with the terrorist in question. These were found written beside the fallen Inspector."

The agent didn't mention what was used for "ink" to write those words, though everyone knew.

"While handwriting evidence is inconclusive, there is enough similarity to ascertain it is likely to have been written by the same man who committed the previous attacks.

"The second piece of evidence is a large bag of the drug LSD left on the scene. And the third is a piece of strap that was found clutched in the hand of Inspector Riley."

As Agent Gibson was finally able to wind down from the intense focus of his presentation, a tiny bit of his Alabama roots unconsciously peeked through.

"I thank y'all for your attention and direct y'all to Forensics Specialist Neil Kendricks-Johnson, who will discuss our analysis of this here evidence found on the scene. I now turn the floor over to my esteemed colleague, with whom I prepared this report and presentation."

And the large, black shadow cast by the dark, Jeri-curl-wearing "Professor" filled the room as he stood, making the room feel smaller.

It was the day after Christmas, and tomorrow the city would bury a hero – a man by the name of Patrick Halloran Riley. And, that too, would cast a large shadow....

70

The average prison correctional officer in the state of Ohio earns $43,360. Salaries typically start from $35,250 and go up to $51,460. Nationally, around one out of every six correctional officers leave their jobs every year.

Being a prison guard is considered to be a low pay, low esteem, high stress, high burnout job. On a daily basis, a prison guard has to see, process, and emotionally absorb experiences that most people witness only occasionally in movies.

Correctional Officer Keandre Hatch had been working at the Ohio State Penitentiary for six months. This was long enough for him to already acquire enough relative "seniority" to be assigned to the maximum security ward securing a certain very high-profile suspect.

A suspect with a distinctive and now infamous scar on his face.

Hatch was making his rounds. It was three am.

As he unlocked the door to aisle three, he already had a bad feeling. There was no reason for him to have this feeling and there was every reason for him to have this feeling.

He slowly but confidently checked each cell to answer

three questions:

Are they there?

Are they alive?

Are they up to anything?

The answer to the third question was always "yes", and regular, unscheduled cell inspections would invariably uncover all manner of contraband – makeshift weapons from scraps of plastic or pork chop bones, miniature moonshine stills made from Coke cans, and sex toys made from anything and everything.

But, tonight, his rounds were only to ensure inmates were present, alive, and not doing something so obvious that a brief peer into a cage would reveal it.

A slight, dark, wiry man, with a chip on his shoulder and just enough inner cruelty to be taken seriously, Hatch went from cage to cage, silently this evening, his flash-light beam probing between the bars for evidence that the person who's supposed to be in there was, in fact, in there.

And, still breathing.

The fourth cage on the left, however, was different.

It was almost like something silently vibrated and emanated from within it, like the lingering soundless echo in your head after getting slapped real hard.

There was nothing out of the ordinary that his five senses could pick up at all.

We have more than five senses.

Hatch approached the cell on the left, the one with the vibration, from the far right edge of the hall — or at least as far to the edge as he could safely go and still be out of reach of the prisoner caged in the cell on that side.

He looked into the vibrating cage.

And saw feet.

At eye level.

Two bare feet.

He'd seen this before.

He hadn't seen this before.

It was always and never the same.

He continued peering into the last three remaining, unexamined cages before unlocking the cage with the hanging feet. What had been a very high-profile prisoner hung there lifeless now, his face bruised, bloodied, and purple.

Dead.

Obviously dead.

Hatch pulled out his phone to notify the On-Call Duty Officer.

"This is Hatch. I'm in cell four, aisle three, in max'. Got a hanging, Ob' d. Right. Right. That's the guy. Yeah. That's him. Uh huh. Uh huh. I'll stay here to keep him company until the medical and chaplain arrive. Uh huh. Yup. Blue. Black and blue. Everyone else is in their crib.

Ok. Ok. I will be here. Out."

In six months, Hatch would be one of the 16% of Correctional Officers who leave their position each year.

71

U.S. Department of Justice

 Federal Bureau of Prisons

P R O G R A M S T A T E M E N T

OPI: CPD/CPB

NUMBER: 5553.08

DATE: January 4, 2017

Escapes/Deaths Notifications

Immediately, upon an inmate's death, the Warden (or designee) assembles the following

information concerning the deceased inmate:

 -Name, register number, date of birth.

 -Offense and sentence.

 -Date, time, and location of death.

 -Apparent cause of death.

 -Investigative steps being taken, if necessary.

 -Names and address of survivor or designee.

 -Notifications made.

-Status of autopsy request.

-Brief medical summary related to death.

72

The official cause of death of one Raymond Giuseppe Cardibello would eventually be declared "Suicide by Hanging." The fact that this "suicide" followed Cardibello apparently beating himself about the head and shoulders and sodomizing himself with a toilet plunger raised not an eyebrow.

73

"Lysergic acid diethylamide (LSD), colloquially referred to as acid, is a semisynthetic product of lysergic acid", Neil Kendricks-Johnson, aka "the Professor", began his presentation to the rest of the investigative team by reading the PowerPoint slide, word for word, in a thin reedy voice that belied his large frame.

"It is a serotonergic psychedelic compound that falls under the family of psychedelic drugs. These are powerful psychoactive substances that produce an altered state of consciousness characterized by changes in mood accompanied by distortions of perception, hallucinations, ecstasy, and numerous cognitive processes.

"They have been known to induce mystical or transcendental experience for thousands of years, and have a long association of use for religious and spiritual reasons. It is also used as a recreational drug. LSD is typically either swallowed or held under the tongue. It is often sold on blotter paper, a sugar cube, or gelatin. It can also be injected, insufflated, inserted vaginally or anally.

"LSD is not addictive. However, adverse psychiatric reactions such as anxiety, paranoia, and delusions are possible. LSD is in the ergoline family. LSD is sensitive to oxygen, ultraviolet light, and chlorine, though it may last for years if it is stored away from light and moisture at low temperature. In pure form it is odorless, crystalline, and clear or white in color. As little as 20–30 micrograms can produce an effect."

The Professor turned off the projector.

"Ok, I got all of that right from Wikipedia. We all know what LSD is," and some smirked, and someone coughed, but no one was sure exactly how to take that unexpected reveal.

"None of you need me to teach you what LSD is. I am here, however, to discuss the large bag of it, found on the roof of the Garrett A. Morgan Water Treatment Plant beside the fallen body of Inspector Riley. I will discuss the potential origins of this drug, how it may have been manufactured, what its intended us was, and then the implications to our investigation."

Reedy voice or no, the Professor never needed to read off PowerPoint slides to make a presentation.

74

"What damage a terrorist attack would cause from poisoning a reservoir with LSD is largely unknown," the Professor spoke now without notes or PowerPoint. "During the Cold War, in the 1950s and 60s, the CIA was VERY interested in, some say obsessed with, the effects such an attack might have. They eventually contacted a Los Angeles psychiatrist who had been using LSD in his practice to find out. That psychiatrist's name was Dr. Nick Bercel.

"The CIA asked Dr. Bercel to conduct experiments on just how much LSD would be necessary to dose Los Angeles' water supply with LSD. His conclusion was that the chlorine in the water would neutralize the LSD, rending the attack harmless, and that was that…"

"So, maybe this Other character isn't so smart after all," a voice in the back that no one ever took credit for interrupted.

"I was going to say, 'that was that…or so the CIA wanted people to think'," the reeded instrument that was the Professor's voice continued. "There was a lot of talk at the time, rumors of rumors, that the CIA was busy developing an LSD formula that wasn't neutralized by chlorine. A person with the right connections and some dark web familiarity could likely obtain this formula, if such a formula truly exists."

Out of respect to the spooks in the room, the Professor

was keeping certain parts of his report discrete, while alluding to additional information he might be aware of that could be obtained through additional questioning… if it became necessary.

"In addition to the much-rumored chlorine-resistant LSD formula, there's also the tale of Dr Jim Ketchum. In 1969, Dr. Ketchum was Department Chief in the US Army's program for testing the military effectiveness of psychedelic chemicals. He entered his office one Monday morning and found a black steel barrel in the corner.

"Dr Ketchum assumed there was a good reason for its presence, but after a couple of days he became curious. One evening, he waited until everyone else in the building had gone home and opened the lid.

"The barrel was filled with sealed glass canisters 'like cookie jars'. He took one out to inspect it; the label indicated that the jar contained three pounds of pure EA 1729. This wouldn't mean much to most people, but to anyone working in the field the code was instantly familiar.

"The EA designation indicated the canisters were from the Army's Edgewood Arsenal; EA 1729 is the military designation for LSD. All the other glass canisters were the same, perhaps 14 of them in all. This was enough acid for several hundred million doses with, Ketchum estimated, a street value of over a billion dollars.

"He considered taking all sorts of actions – reporting it, asking superiors, taking a canister for … what? But, ultimately, he did nothing and by the next Friday morning the black steel barrel had vanished as mysteriously as it arrived.

"Or so the legend goes." The Professor was also a good story-teller.

"Here's what we do know. The Garret A. Morgan Water Treatment Plant holds roughly 56,781,176.8 liters in its reservoir. If we assume that each person in the community were to drink the equivalent of two liters in one day, then to toxify the drinking water would require enough LSD to dose 28,390,588.4 liters.

"The threshold dose of LSD is approximately 10 micrograms. Ten micrograms per dose times 28,390,588.4 doses required equals .2839059 kilograms. Roughly six tenths of a pound."

Cleveland's Police Chief was first to connect the dots, "Or almost exactly the amount left behind on the roof."

Suddenly, the attempted attack on the water supply seemed less far-fetched, and the heroics of the late Officer Riley even more heroic.

"Yes," the Professor confirmed. "Or almost exactly the amount left behind on the roof."

75

"The street value of that much LSD must be nearly 20 million dollars," Agent Brandon offered as calmly as citing the price of a gallon of milk. "How would this terrorist acquire that high of a quantity of this drug?" Her tone was as flat as someone asking when the next bus was due.

"We estimate the current street value of that much LSD to be in the neighborhood of 17.5 million dollars," Agent Gibson providing the answer this time. "We do have a theory as to how that much LSD might be obtained."

"There are three avenues we conjecture as potential sources of that much drug." Although the Professor's voice sounded drastically different from Agent Gibson's, their statements flowed together as seamlessly as though they were one person speaking.

"Those avenues are: 1) commercial diversion; 2) organic manufacture; and 3) confiscation diversion," the Professor continued, his voice as squeaky as a dog chew toy, and yet as dominant in the room as his physique.

"First theory: commercial diversion. Approximately 20 tons of lysergic acid, a precursor of LSD, is manufactured legally each year and turned into legitimate medicines, such as nicergoline, a treatment for dementia. An unscrupulous chemistry storeroom clerk could be bribed, and all the legal obstacles to obtaining the precursor drugs to manufacturing LSD could be circumvented. For a modest sum, a person with the right connections could potentially have a 5-gallon container of lysergic acid placed right into the trunk of their car.

"Second theory: organic manufacture. Harvard scientists have shown how simple microbes such as those found in baker's yeast can be modified to make LSD. Once you've got the microorganisms properly genetically modified, LSD potentially becomes as cheap to manufacture as yogurt."

"Of course," the Gibson voice of the seemingly one-person Neil-Kendricks/Gibson duo interjected, "this would require access to a very sophisticated lab and a training in biochemistry, which itself suggests some potential leads."

"There are precedents for large-scale manufacturing labs," the Professor continued. "In 2000, William Leonard Pickard and Clyde Apperson were pulled over while driving a Ryder rental truck they were using to move their LSD laboratory across Kansas. This led to the largest LSD drug bust in history. The laboratory, which had been stored near a renovated Atlas-E missile silo near Wamego, Kansas, was capable of creating a kilo of LSD every five weeks.

"Our third theory is confiscation diversion." The Professor paused here to let that sink in.

"You mean, confiscation by law enforcement agencies," Agent Brandon again was first to connect the dots.

The Professor just nodded. "Virtually anyone in law enforcement could potentially access LSD confiscated in various drug busts, gradually extract quantities from the bust, replace those quantities with some other powder, and, like teens drinking their parents' booze and topping it back up with water, accumulate a significant amount over time."

"So, you're suggesting maybe a dirty cop?'" Cleveland's Police Chief, Calvin D. Williams, wasn't one to mince words.
"That's one theory," Agent Gibson answering this time. "Our current working theory for most likely avenue the terrorist used to obtain the drug is 'all of the above'."

"We believe," the Professor continued, "that it's likely that some of the LSD was diverted, some of it manufactured."

"We come to this conclusion," Gibson again, "from a preliminary examination of the LSD itself. Its composition is very diverse – some is more potent than others, some of a formulation that suggests organic creation, other portions suggest industrial precursors."

"I see." Agent Brandon did see. "So, we are dealing with a very resourceful, patient, intelligent individual who has access to a lab, and connections in both the industrial underground and potentially in law enforcement, as well."

"That sums it up nicely," the Professor answered like a teacher acknowledging a clever student.

"Thank you for an illuminating report, Dr. Kendricks-Johnson," Agent Brandon voice was formal and professional, although her referring to the Professor as "Doctor" was unusual to hear for those in the room.

"Any theories as to what this terrorist hoped to gain by dosing the drinking water with LSD?"

"We do, Agent Brandon," Agent Gibson's voice this time chimed in without hesitation and the large, Black Professor sat down. It was obvious the two had anticipated the questions they would be asked and prepared carefully coordinated responses in advance.

"One word. Fear. Imagine an entire city unexpectedly experiencing hallucinations. While it's unlikely the dose would be so powerful as to render the entire population helpless, the confusion over what was happening would quickly go viral. Especially in this current high state of tension created by the previous attacks.

"Imagine parents across the county seeing their children act bizarrely. Imagine they, themselves, growing confused and frightened over their own inexplicable disorientation. Imagine hospitals over-run with anxiety cases. The source would soon be uncovered, which would only exacerbate the panic as people across the country began to question the safety of their own drinking water."

"This Other terrorist has a messianic drive to create maximum fear, all of it focused on himself." The Professor's turn now, as he stood and Agent Gibson sat – their presentation was well-choreographed.

"The psychological profile of this madman is straightforward. He's obsessed with generating as much fear as he can, fear of himself, in an attempt to otherwise blot out and extinguish all our fears of anyone and anything else.

"He sees himself as a hero in a war…and the people he kills and terrorizes casualties in that war. For him, the territory to be won isn't land, it's the space between people's heads. And in their hearts."

"Is he insane?" Agent Brandon asked.

Agent Gibson and the Professor looked at each other, and then blurted out almost in unison "Oh yes. Very much so."

Jack Wharton had been listening to this report, in silence, with the rest of the group. Only now he felt himself inexplicably uncomfortable, squirming in his chair.

"Any questions?" the Professor asked.

There were questions, though too unformed to be asked just yet. However, in the weeks and days ahead they would surely be posed. Right now, the room of trained investigators silently mulled over in their minds the significance of what they'd just heard.

"Then, that concludes the LSD investigation portion of our presentation. We've yet to ascertain if the LSD found on the roof had been modified to be resistant to chlorine," the Professor wrapped up. "Agent Gibson will now report on the second significant piece of evidence – the piece of strap discovered in Officer Riley's hand."

76

The bureaucracies in law enforcement function pretty much like the departments in any other large industry or profession. Information tends to move in silos, where reports are sent up the chain of command within each jurisdiction's organizational tunnel, and then, once the information reaches the top of the chain, it only then get transferred laterally to other departments and agencies.

The information then goes in reverse – it moves downward from the top of the other silo, down the various levels, until it finally reaches the level in the second department that needs to know it.

That dynamic applies even when the information that needs to be shared is that a suspected terrorist just hung himself.

77

"This is the strap that was discovered in Officer Riley's hand," Agent Gibson pulled out a piece of elastic strap, about six inches long, from a plastic evidence bag. "It appears to be from an article of clothing or perhaps some specialized active gear – perhaps from a brace or piece of camping or sports equipment. You can see that it looks old and worn." He passed it around.

"It's okay for you all to touch it. It's been tested for

DNA." The mood in the room brightened briefly, and then darkened into confusion upon hearing "Nothing."

"How could someone wear a strap and not leave any DNA?" Jack Wharton's voice for the first time, which surprised him most of all.

"Two factors. One, the strap was initially wiped clean of DNA through a sanitizing agent, probably bleach. Two, the strap must never have come in contact with the terrorist's skin. If you'll look at this slide," and the projector came on, "you can see traces of a black, micro-fiber mesh. We believe this is what the terrorist was wearing under whatever garment this piece of strap came from."

"What would have been the intended purpose of wearing this mesh undergarment?" Agent Brandon was making a habit of asking the most pertinent questions.

"We have two theories," Agent Gibson had theories. When you graduate top of your class from Alabama's Regis University Master of Science in Criminology program, you're never short of theories. "Our first theory is that he wore this mesh undergarment as a form of nighttime concealment. The second theory is that he wore a full-body mesh undergarment with the specific intent of not leaving behind any DNA evidence. Or both."

"Thank you. Proceed." Agent Brandon was always tracking.

"Please, everyone, if you don't already have a piece of paper and something to write with in front of you, please do so now. As you pass the strap around, I ask you to use your imagination, your instincts. Don't even hesitate. Whatever first comes to mind, make note of it. Right now. Capture it. Write it down. No matter how absurd. Instincts are our first source of investigative direction," Agent Gibson was well-schooled.

And, the team did as directed – each member, in turn, handled the piece of strap like the remains of an alien visitor from another planet. Stretching it, pulling it, holding it up to the light, rubbing it against their cheek, rolling it into a ball – and then writing, writing, anything that came to mind. Anything that might lead to the right door.

Once the strap had circulated the room, Agent Gibson asked, "How many wrote down jock strap?". A few hands. Then a few more. Then, nearly all of them.

"Good. Shows you weren't self-censoring your brainstorming. Of course, we will also pursue leads more methodically – closely examining every piece of athletic, camping, and support gear we can find. But, parallel to that investigation, we will also be tracking down every single thought you just wrote down."

"Anything else on this strap, Agent?" Brandon was about to regain the reins.

"Only that the strap appears to be worn, and seems to have been used extensively for its originally designed purpose."

"Thank you, Agent Gibson and Dr. Hendricks-Johnson. The next step, then, is to assign members to our four investigative teams: 1) Team LSD; 2) Team Cardibello;

3) Team Strap; and 4) Team Video."

And, teams were assigned. Buddy O' Malley volunteered for all four teams, but was told that two would be the limit to ensure no one was stretched too thin. Chief Williams was first to volunteer for Team Cardibello. Jack Wharton volunteered for Team Strap and Team Video.

Something about that strap pawed at his mind like a dog scratching at a door to go out and do his business.

So, the 12 members leading the investigative team formed four teams of three members each. Each team member would be expected to deliver the full resources available from the department or organization they represented.

Something about that strap….

A knock on the door. Urgent. Insistent.

Agent Brandon was not amused. Her glare would have incinerated the knocker had they not been shielded by the wood of the door.

A second knock. Equally insistent.

Brandon nodded her head one inch.

The nearest team member sprang to their feet and answered. The knocker who'd been spared Brandon's lasers by the door's wooden protection was the intern, Marcy Meadows. Every jaw in the room clenched, but before the obligatory ass-chewing could commence, the desperate words flowed out from the intern.

"You need to turn on the news! Ray Cardibello is dead!

Hung himself in prison!" And she stood there like a pizza delivery person waiting for a tip.

The projector switched to a silent broadcast of the news, and sure enough, there was a picture of the penitentiary with the chyron "Once Lead Suspect of 'Other' Massacre Found Hung in Prison."

"What is your name, Ms.?" Agent Brandon asked, as politely as speaking to someone who had just offered her their seat on the bus.

Breathless response. "Marcy Meadows! Ma'am!"

"Thank you, Ms. Meadows. You've done well. You are excused."

And Ms. Meadows gratefully disappeared, bowing and backing out of the room.

"Team Cardibello will have a summary update report on the circumstances surrounding Cardibello's death within one hour. After that, the members of Team Cardibello will re-assign themselves into the other three investigative teams so that we have now will three focus teams of four members each."

Chief Williams sat there silently with his face in lockjaw mode, clenching his fists. He'd felt in his bones that Cardibello knew ... something. Now, that something secret locked away, buried forever, outside his reach.

Agent Brandon stood up, briskly put her documents and devices into an organized set of carrying cases, all of which seemed to fit together like Russian nesting dolls, and announced, "Lady and gentlemen, we have work to do. Dismissed."

And, she stepped out like a sheriff in a western leaving a bar after stopping the bad guy in the black hat.

And, Jack Wharton's mind kept twisting like the tail of a kite…or like a random piece of athletic strap, billowing in the wind.

78

Jack Wharton was in his late-twenties, or at least he was wearing the same mullet-inspired 'do he wore when he was of that age. He was floating, flowing, atop a shiny, shiny mirror. The mirror was rectangular, maybe 200 feet long and nearly 100 feet wide, by Jack's reckoning. A mirror shiny, with a thin fog wafting above it…like a graveyard scene from a horror movie.

The mirror he was flowing atop was surrounded by people, sitting in rows of chairs, watching and hollering, screaming, bellowing – he could see their mouths wide open, their fists manically pumping into the air, flags waving about, a section of band members – all wearing identical tall white hats and double-breasted navy blue coats – playing vigorously. He could see grinning children with malicious grins, chewing identical grey somethings on a stick…but, he couldn't hear a sound.

He floated along on this mirror, witnessing without hearing, in the center stage of what should have been a cacophony of noise, but instead was silent and still.

A breeze billowed up a spider web of fog that lazily spiraled and eddied around him.

He eventually came upon a cage with white bars and positioned himself in front of it. As he floated along to turn his back to the cage, he thought he caught a glimpse of something…something that looked like two legs that were themselves floating, only what he thought he might have seen were the bottom halves of legs – just from the knee down – and they seemed to be floating from the top of the small cage into the center of it.

Somehow, Jack knew he didn't have time to examine the floating legs, or even confirm he'd actually seen them, as he was just about to have work to do. Work that would start any second.

Just then, from the far end of the rectangle, appeared in the fog, box-shaped human figures that floated along the top of the mirror like ghosts. They approached in a winding single-file line, looking like a snake would look if it were a moving, connect-the-dots puzzle. Identical, fuzzy, unfocused, floating, box-shaped ghosts, drifting back and forth across the mirror…closer and closer to Jack and his white cage.

"Thwwwipppp!" an object – something lacking any identifiable shape — came flying at Jack, traveling at great speed, from the nearest floating ghost.

Just before the unidentifiable object could strike Jack, he was able to deploy a shield (which he now suddenly had) and deflect the morphing, tan-colored projectile.

The ghost who'd fired this projectile then floated back

to the end of the snake queue, and the second ghost approached.

"Thwwwaaap!" and again, a shape-shifting object, spinning and twisting in air like a snake itself, came firing from the second ghost, this time to Jack's immediate right. Just at the last instant, as before, Jack was able to thrust his shield and deflect it.

And the second ghost silently floated to the back of the dotted "snake" atop the giant mirror.

Over and over again, the ghostly, floating box-shapes would approach from the front of the snake-line and "thwwip!" fire a tan, snake piece at him, and each time, he would somehow place his shield in the projectile's path and deflect it, rendering it harmless.

The people in the audience began to shape-shift themselves, as did Jack's clothing. At some point, while he was focused on using his shield to protect both himself and the floating legs he thought he'd seen in the white cage behind him, he found himself wearing his old Navy uniform.

When that happened – when his clothing was no longer what he would wear in his late 20s, but instead became the military garb he'd worn only a few years earlier — the crowd stopped its antic, silent gestures.

Instead of wild gesticulating, each member of the audience took out a mirror, and put it in front of their faces – and each mirror showed Jack's face, so that as Jack looked up and around – in those few moments in between blocking projectiles when he could avert his eyes – all he could see, all he could see, as far as he could see was his own face…staring back at him.

All he could see. All he could see. All he could see.

Mirrors. His own face staring at him.

Jack was becoming exhausted, and knew he couldn't keep this up much longer. His shield was breaking, cracking into pieces. As was his will.

And still, the relentless, snaking queue of ghosts floated back and forth before him, firing their projectile snakes … and then coasting to the back of the line, showing not the least bit of frustration or exhaustion themselves.

Jack came up with a plan. A longshot. Something he wasn't sure he could do, but would try, and just his thinking of this new strategy brought the crowd back to life, only this time he could hear them!

He could hear them bellowing and shouting – a roar like a subway train rushing by without stopping – they began throwing their handheld mirrors at the giant mirror Jack and the box-ghosts were floating on, and the small mirrors, as they fell, began to make cracks in the larger mirror.

As the next ghost-box approached, Jack somehow ran at it! Ran straight at it atop the cloudy mirror surface…10 feet away, now 8…the ghost-box was still swaying back and forth, getting into position, and finally, just as it was about to fire away, just as it was about to fire away, Jack leaped at it, leaped with all his might…and, as he soared to tackle the ghost, he could see the clothes the ghost was actually wearing, could see the uniform all the ghosts were all wearing… the uniform of a Cleveland Police officer…

… when he struck the ghost, it vanished in smoke…and each of the other ghost-boxes in turn went up in smoke, and each of the audience members went up in smoke, and the cage that might have once contained two floating half-legs, it went up in smoke, and the fog atop the mirror lifted, and the cracks all healed, and Jack could see in the mirror clearly…

…and the mirror he was now sprawled atop, 200 feet long and nearly 100 feet wide, showed one image… Jack's face.

Jack looked down and saw something else directly in front of him. He saw what the ghost-boxes in Cleveland Police Officer uniforms had been firing at him.

A bit of elastic fabric. A piece of strap…about six inches long….

By now, Jack was used to what he called his "Fireball gargle" – the belt he'd take when he found himself lying in his bed, covered with sweat. He wouldn't just drink it, he'd swish it in his mouth and gargle with the sweet liquor, before swallowing it.

He picked up his phone.

"Hei. Kuka siellä on?" Sometimes, when bi-lingual people are awakened out of a deep sleep to answer the phone, they aren't always clear-headed enough to choose the language that comes out. FBI Agent Sjoltsen

Vinjrud was no exception.

"Hi Vineyard. This is Jack." Jack's voice was a gravely grinder, but he used Vinrud's nickname to identify himself.

"Vat? What? Jack? Jack…Varton, Wharton?"

"Yep. Good morning."

"Morning? What's (yawn) the time?"

"I think it's around 3 am. Look, sorry to wake you up, but I just had…just had a thought…."

"You had a thought at 3 am and your thought was … to call me? Please, humor me by having different thoughts in the future."

"Sorry about that, but this is important. How soon can you open up the video lab and provide access to the surveillance files?"

"Surveillance files? You mean…from the Rapid attack? …I was planning on coming in at 8?"

"Can you make it sooner?"

"How soon?"

"Now?"

Silence.

"I had a thought. My thought was that you'd say that." It was hard to tell if Vinrud was annoyed, amused, or both.

"I can be at the office in 30 minutes, but Jack?"

"Yah, Vineyard?"

"Please to stop calling me 'Vineyard'."

79

Jack Wharton was sober. Maybe as sober as he'd ever been in his entire life. Sitting in the special investigations computer lab at the downtown Cleveland Police Station, he'd just spent hours pouring over the same video, over and over … even though what he suspected he'd find was apparent in just the first few minutes.

It was 7:30 am. and in walked Sjoltsen Vinjrud, wearing a light grey suit with tight legs and a tight-fitting jacket, a white shirt, no tie, and a 5 o' clock shadow that wasn't intentional today.

"Find what you were looking for?" Vinjrud had just finished a light breakfast. He stepped out after he let his impetuous American colleague into the secure computer lab and opened the files he'd requested.

Jack stared at the screen as he spoke. "Did you ever see that video," he began, "where you're supposed to watch a group of basketball players who are bouncing a basketball between them in a circle?"

Vinjrud could sense an intense poignancy in Jack's voice. And said nothing.

"The video asks the viewer to count how many times the players bounce the ball between them. You ever see that video?"

"No, Jack, I haven't."

"Well, there's a catch. I watched that video, and I counted the bounces, and I even got the number right. But, you know what I didn't see? What I didn't see was a man dressed up in a gorilla suit who quite clearly and slowly walked between and around the basketball players. I only even realized the gorilla was there after I was told to watch the video again, only this time, to look for the gorilla.

"I honestly couldn't believe it. I couldn't believe I could stare at a video with a man in a gorilla suit walking around a group of basketball players and not even see him! He was invisible to me… because I wasn't looking for a man in a gorilla suit. I was looking to count bounces.

"It was so obvious. My first thought was that the video was somehow altered – that it couldn't possibly be real. That there was no way I could not see the image right in front of me. But, there it was… invisible right in front of my eyes…because I was looking for something else… my brain was blind to the gorilla."

Vinjrud paused, and asked, "Jack, do you see our gorilla now?"

"You know, Vinjrud, I like you. You're smart. You're detailed. Dedicated. But, even the brightest mind, even the most dedicated investigator is going to miss that gorilla…if they're watching the bouncing ball instead.

"I believe I've got my gorilla spotted right here, Vinjrud," and Jack held up a flash drive. "Now, I'm going to put him in a cage."

"You're not going to show me." Vinjrud's question was more of a statement – he already knew the answer.

Jack got up.

"What's next?"

"Next," Jack answered, "I'm going to pick up a certain strap from the evidence room…and then, I'm going to have a conversation with a gorilla."

"I don't think you can walk out with a critical piece of evidence like that, Jack."

"You ever hear 'where there's a will, there's a way'?" and Jack smiled, sort of.

Jack reached out his hand.

"Oh, by the way, thanks for all your help. Sorry about waking you up…sometimes, I don't sleep too well…and sorry about that 'Vineyard' stuff too?"

And, with that, they shook hands, and Jack walked out.

"Americans," Vinjrud said, and he sat down in the same chair Jack had just been sitting in. And started looking at the same video files Jack had been watching – the same files he, himself, had watched over and over again… only this time, he'd be looking for that gorilla.

80

"I've been waiting for you."

Jack was sitting in "his" chair in the Berea Batcave when his lifelong partner, Johnson, came in.

"Oh. Okay, well, wait no longer! Your partner is here! Any progress on the case? Wanna' beer?"
"No, Johnson, I have some things to show you."

"About the case? Don't tell me my partner is about to be a hero for the second time? Damn! Maybe, this time you'll get a call from the pope! Have you canonized as a saint while you're still around. Wouldn't that be something? My partner. Saint Jack!"

"Sit down, Johnson."

"What's this all about?"

"Please, just sit down."

And, Johnson, confused, sat down.

"Do you recognize this?" Jack held out the piece of elastic strap that had been discovered in the hand of a dead security officer atop a reservoir.

"That looks like the evidence strap you've shown me pictures of in the 'Other' case. Building yourself a jock? ...wait, how'd you get it? Don't tell me my partner is tampering with evidence? Well, that's no way for a saint to act. Hey, let me get us a couple cool ones...."

But, Johnson's attempt to stand was halted by a single word spoken in a singular way.

"Sit."

Johnson sat.

"Say, what's this all about, partner. Why so serious today?"

"Do you recognize this?"

"Sure, like I said, it's the key piece of evidence in the 'Other' case. What you're doing with it is beyond me. Why do you keep asking? Don't you know what it is?"

"Have you ever seen it before?"

"When before? How could I see this piece of evidence before? You know I never go into the office."

"I'm not talking about the office, Johnson. I'm talking about before."

"Before…what?"

"I know you did it."

"Did it? Did what? Drink your last beer?"

"Why?"

"Why? Because I was thirsty. Have you gone crazy?"

"So, if I were to suggest that this piece of strap is actually from a piece of athletic equipment, a piece of athletic equipment we both had access to, you wouldn't know anything about that?"

"I have no idea what the hell you are talking about, but

please… enlighten me."

"Let's suppose I were to get a bolt cutter and open the locker where you keep your athletic gear, right in the back room there. What do you think I'd find?"

"Uhhhh, athletic equipment?"

"True. True. And perhaps, one piece of athletic equipment in particular. A particular old-school hockey mask. Only this hockey mask would have one broken strap…a strap that precisely fit this strap here in my hand, what would you say to that?"

Silence.

"What would you further say if I suggested that, in that same locker, I would find my old hockey goalie equipment modified into a functioning armored undergarment for combat? What would you say to that suggestion?"

"Well, I would say I'm not sure what's in that damn locker, but I would say that there are a lot of people who could potentially put something in that locker. This building isn't exactly Fort Knox."

"Of course you would. Please look at this monitor."

"Kathy does Cleveland?"

"You'll see here some of the key footage captured on surveillance cameras right after the 'Other' planted a bomb on the downtown Rapid Transit car."

"Seen it a thousand times. Come on, Jack, reruns? Really? I mean, the entertainment value…."

"And, as we have discussed a thousand times, the home-less-looking terrorist is last scene here," and Jack froze the image and closed in, "at point Z, on exit camera 7C. He stumbles off into this hallway carrying a bag. He does not come out."

"Jack. We've been over and over this."

"Every other person who is seen entering that hallway, on every video, is also seen leaving on other video. And no one else who didn't go in that hallway comes out."

"Maybe, he's a ghost."

"Or maybe, he's a gorilla."

"A what?"

"Johnson, I ask you to look at this image here," and he freeze-framed an image of a man leaving the hallway. "Do you recognize this person?"

"Yes, handsome devil I'd say. That's me!"

"Yes, that is definitely a picture of you. A picture of you in your police uniform carrying a bag. Walking out of the passageway. The passageway that the 'Other' walked into and did not walk out of.

"Only there is no image of you ever entering that hall-way. No one ever noticed that it was you, in your police uniform, who walked out of that hallway...but did not walk in...or rather, you did walk in...dressed in the clothing of a homeless man.

"And, we never, ever noticed it was you, because no one –

not the video specialists, the FBI, the NSA, the brightest scientists enhancing every pixel of every image – no one was looking for a cop to come out of that hallway. A cop that didn't walk in. Your police uniform was the gorilla costume that made you invisible, Johnson.

"You are the 'Other' we've all been looking for."

"Nice piece of police work, partner, but now what are you going to do?'

"You have the right to remain silent…."

"Hahahaha! You can't be serious!"

"You're under arrest, Johnson."

"You might think I'm under arrest, but you're not stopping me… partner! You're can't stop me. Firstly, what I'm doing is right!"

"What!?! Killing innocent people is 'right'? What the fuck, Johnson! You're a terrorist! You're like goddamn bin Laden, motherfucker! You're BUSTED!"

"Look," and Johnson stood up and calmly walked to the window and looked outside. "Look out there, Jack. What do you see?"

"I see a world that's going to be a whole lot safer without scum like you living in it."

Johnson looked down and smiled before returning his gaze to outside the window, where a cold, unrelenting Cleveland snow storm was just starting to show its teeth.

"You look outside, Jack, really look, and you'll admit

you see what we all see. We see fear. We see hate. We see bigotry. People judging each other by the color of their skin. We see people fearing and hating and attacking old men because they're wearing turbans. We see people hollering at a Mexican woman standing on the bus with her children – 'speak American' – they holler, 'go home!'

"We see a world where families fleeing for their lives are rejected – cast aside to die – because they have brown skin from a different country and practice a different religion. We see Black men across the country shot by cops – cops like us – with no consequence whatsoever – so fearful are we of Black men we overlook the real danger – people like us who can kill innocent people for no reason and get away with it."

"And, your solution is to go psycho terrorist? That's going to fix everything. Dude, you are fucked up."

"It's WORKING! Don't you see?!? It's goddamn working! You see people out there now – they don't care if you're Black, brown, white, yellow, red, or blue! They're scared now, all right! But, they are scared TOGETHER! They're have found the means to bond together against a common foe, ONE Other. One fear!

"Look outside again. Right now, look! There's Mr. McCain. The Vietnam vet'. Right now, he's going over to the Greens house – that's right, the Black family – and you know what he's doing? He's on volunteer escort watch for the block and he's walking Mrs. Green to the bus stop. And he's going to stay there with her until the bus comes.

"You think that old Marine is packin'? You bet your balls he is. You think, right now, he's thinking all that 'nigger this' and 'nigger that' bullshit he usually spouts at the bar? NO! In their common fear – their shared fear – their shared fear of ME – he's found the means to look beyond the skin color to see a person, a neighbor, a human being…like himself. Not an 'other'. A 'same'. I helped cure him, Jack. I'm helping to cure and free everyone of fear!"

"You have the right to an attorney…."

"And, you know who else is the 'other', Jack? We are! We cops most of all."

"Don't put your blood on my hands, you psycho!"

"But, it's already on your hands. And my hands. And the hands of all us who are sworn as police officers to 'protect and serve'."

And Johnson slumped against the window frame and wept.

"That 12-year-old boy. Remember what we were doing at 12, Jack? Remember the hood? When I came into your life? Twelve years old. Tamir Rice. Shot by one of our own. Shot by a man wearing the same exact uniform we wear – the same exact uniform I had on when I walked out that tunnel.

"Emotionally unfit for duty. That's what they said about the cop that killed that boy. He was deemed emotionally unstable and unfit for duty when he was a cop in Independence. Didn't mention that on his application. No one checked. Just came screeching up to some kid, some BLACK kid, jumped out, and killed him…cuz he was by himself playing with a toy guy.

"His sister was there. She ran to his aid. What did the cops do? They held her down. Didn't call for an ambulance right away. They tried to arrest his sister.

"What did the city of Cleveland do? They tried to bill the family for the ambulance. Six million dollars doesn't make up for your son getting shot and killed, Jack. You think I'm a monster? Any system that lets a guy like that get away with shooting and killing a kid is the monster."

Click.

The sound of the handcuffs going on Johnson's wrist was familiar to both of them.

"I said you can't arrest me, Jack."

"You have the right to an attorney…"

"I'm walking out of here right now, Jack. I'm walking out of here and I'm going to continue doing what I've been doing. I'm going to continue doing it, only next stop will be Pittsburgh. No, San Diego. It's nice there this time of year. Only, first, I'm going to stop by my locker to pick up … a few items."

And, with that, Johnson started to walk away. He was handcuffed and yet he was walking away. Jack pulled his gun.

"Oh, you can't shoot me either."

"Halt! Halt or I'll shoot!"

But, Johnson didn't halt.

"Last warning! Don't make me kill you!"

Johnson was nearly out of the room.

BANG!

And the .40 caliber bullet from Jack's Glock 22 thundered through the room…and the sound of glass shattering…of the world shattering…of everything shattering….

…shiny bits of broken reality twinkled in the air, afloat and drifting to the ground like dying butterflies stricken in mid-flight….

…adrift, adrift, like dust motes floating along on the smoke from his gun…

…sprinkling to the ground like glistening colored snowflakes, like the snowflakes falling outside….

…Jack's world was a kaleidoscope. It seemed to spin into colorful shapes unknowing and yet entrancing…

…the world was confetti, floating around…inside a rainbow snow globe freshly shaken…

…and the din gradually faded…and the confetti all fell to the ground, and the shards of his broken reality with it…

…and the world became clear. As clear as the surface of the moon through a telescope.

He could see clearly what was before him.

A mirror.

A mirror broken into pieces by the bullet he'd fired into it.

In the remaining reflective glass, however, he could still see enough of what was before him. An image. An image of one man. A man with a handcuff on each wrist and holding a handgun. A handgun pointed at the mirror.

He could see his own image.

The image of the only man in the room.

81

FRANKLIN MEDICAL CENTER

OHIO DEPARTMENT OF REHABILITATION AND CORRECTION

COLUMBUS, OHIO

"So, all these Other murders were committed by Jack Wharton's imaginary partner, is that what you're telling me?" Cleveland's Chief of Police Calvin D. Williams thought he had seen and heard everything. Every lie, delusion, excuse, alibi, cover story, bizarre behavior, mental illness, violent act, and just plain weirdness anyone could imagine – he thought he'd seen it all in his 46 years on the force, nine on the SWAT team.

But, this was something he honestly had a hard time accepting. It was just too … crazy.

"Well, his partner was real to him. Really 'inside'

him. Really a part of him. The murderer was actually another personality that existed inside of him, but the short answer, Chief, is yes, that's what it boils down to in the end." Neil Kendricks-Johnson had just spent two hours being briefed by the elite team of psychotherapists assigned to assess, diagnose, and treat their newest patient – a famous member of the Cleveland Police Force named Jack Wharton.

"What the hell, Neil," the Chief almost never called his associate by his first name, "I thought that multiple personalities stuff was only in movies, like zombies and vampires. How can this be…real?"

"Honestly, that's what I always thought too, Chief," even after being called "Neil", there was no way he was going to call the Chief "Samuel." "But, it turns out, while multiple personalities this distinct are extremely rare, dissociative identity disorder – the technical term for 'multiple personalities' – actually occurs in approximately two percent of the population."

Kendricks-Johnson and Chief Williams just stared into each other's eyes, both holding questions that couldn't be answered – questions about how we know what's real, and what we really know about the person we see when we look in the mirror…and how anyone might behave if that mirror somehow cracked. Or opened into the other side of the looking glass. And they fell in.

They were joined in a private interview office by FBI Agent Thomas Gibson, who stood to the side, present but also giving the two other men space to process what had happened to their long-time friend and fellow officer. He had completed a thesis on dissociative disorder at Alabama's Regis University, but refrained from chiming in out of respect for his colleagues.

It had only been two days since a neighbor of Wharton's called the police with a report of having heard a gunshot. The officers who answered that call were, themselves, receiving counseling to help them manage the experience of having seen a fellow officer in complete psychotic break, holding a conversation with himself, in two different voices … one hand handcuffed to the other…his weapon menacingly pointed at a mirror…a mirror shattered by a single bullet hole in the center.

"How, Neil, how?" the Chief's organized mind needed an explanation – a place in his head that he could somehow file all this in a way that made some kind of sense.

"Ninety percent of people with dissociative disorder have experienced childhood trauma. That's what happened to Jack. Part of what I'm about to tell now was explained by Jack, and some was told from his other personality, someone he calls 'Johnson.' So, this explanation is like a story interpreted from an archaeological expedition – pieced together by the team of therapists who have been treating him fairly intensively, and digging up clues, since Jack arrived.

"Jack grew up in Murray Hill, and as a child had a rough time of it."

"Hmph. Murray Hill." The Chief had little to say that was positive of the Murray Hill neighborhood, especially "back in the day" – its reputation for threatening and abusing Black people was something he was well aware of, personally.

"The only Jewish kid in the neighborhood, he mostly kept to himself. Lonely. Scared. Essentially friendless. One night, he witnesses a horrific act – the brutal death of an African-American boy at the hands of gang members."

"Fucking Ambassadors scum."

"Yes, Chief. It was them. And the person who committed this murder? Our old friend, Ray Cardibello. That's how he got the scar."

Another "hmph."

"Turns out, Jack just sat there and watched this kid get beaten to death and did nothing. Said nothing. Saw a boy get beaten to death just because of the color of his skin right in front of him…and just sat there, forever silent about it…until now.

"So, he's just a kid himself, by himself, tortured with guilt. Unable to accept that he just sat there and did nothing. How does he resolve this? Where can he go with it? What does he do? At one point, he planned to kill himself, and then, somehow, a 'solution' developed.

"That's when 'Johnson' was created, or rather, became more real. Like a lot of lonely kids, he had an imaginary friend he called Johnson – perfectly normal. But, to alleviate the pain of his guilt, he came to blame Johnson for not doing anything. It wasn't HIM that was too cowardly to act – it was 'Johnson'."

"I think many of us in the South do something similar." Agent Gibson spoke up, and his two African-American colleagues were touched by the thoughtfulness of his comment.

"It ain't just the South, Thomas." The Chief had grown to hold a rare respect for Agent Gibson.

"This ultimately worked too well," the Professor continued. "As time went on, 'Johnson' became more and more real, until 'Johnson' became real – a fully-developed personality that, from time to time, would 'come out' – come out and take over.

"That's why he washed out from the SEALs. Eventually, after living and working in close quarters with fellow military, his psychosis became apparent. Ditto with his ex-wife.

"Cardibello knew it too. He didn't just call Jack 'Wart' – he used to call him 'Crazy Wart'. Cardibello had a hunch it was Jack all along – ultimately, he would have testified pointing the finger at Jack, once he could get himself a deal. But, his attorney dragged his feet on arranging any deals, and he was having a hard time getting people to listen to him anyway. He had his own issues, and wasn't the greatest communicator either."

"So, that's why Jack had Cardibello killed – to keep him quiet." The Chief well understood how easy it is for a dirty cop to have someone in prison eliminated, especially if that someone is suspected of committing heinous acts.

"Yes. The only reason Cardibello was even involved in this in the first place is that he just happened to be dumpster-diving in the park when the first murder happened. A paperboy saw him, and with his record…he became the prime suspect pretty quick."

"So, this 'Johnson' personality was latent and self-expressed for years. Why did it manifest itself in violence now?" Gibson spoke up to ask the type of question only someone who had studied the subject would ask, and the two men realized that the FBI agent was holding back out of deference to his colleagues. "Do the doctors have any theories about what triggered all this?"

"Yes, they have a theory. More than a theory, really. An actual motive, right out of the mouth of 'Johnson' himself. It was the Tamir Rice shooting. When a grand jury decided not to bring charges against Timothy Loehmann for shooting the 12-year-old, it reminded Johnson of the murderous beating he'd witnessed as a child. The murder he had done nothing about.

"Now, as an adult, he couldn't stand by and do nothing after watching another Black youth killed for what he felt was no good reason, other than the color of his skin. So, he decided to become a unifying character for good, 'the Other.' He created some improvised body armor from hockey goalie equipment he had lying around, and used his knowledge as a police officer to plan his attacks."

"So, all the time 'Johnson' was killing people as the Other, Wharton was working on solving those murders? The murders he was actually committing?" The Chief was doing a good job concealing just how staggered he was by all this.

"He was a brilliant cop. We're still trying to figure out everything he had in his lab. Apparently, he could even use it to manufacture LSD."

The three men looked out the window. Snow was on the ground. They could see their reflections. The Chief reached into his pocket. He pulled out two hundred-dollar bills.

"We're going to a quiet bar I know. Nice view of the lake. We're not leaving until we spend this."

And, the three men drank the two hundred dollars. In silence at first. Then, in reflection. Then, finally, in boisterous good cheer. That latter part – when they partied like it was New Year's Eve – they couldn't remember a single thing they talked about. But, they did remember they'd be bonded as friends for the rest of their lives.

They'd also remember something else.

A time when someone became the Other...

...became the Other because he never felt part of "us".

That is all.

Epilogue

"How you feeling, Chief?"

"You really have to ask…Professor?"

The two men were torturously hung over. It was Martin Luther King Day and they'd both come in anyway.

"What brings an egghead like you to the Chief of Police's office? And, this better not be anything that makes my head hurt. That would not be well-received."

"It's an envelope, Chief. From the Offices of National Security…it's from Carla Brandon."

"Ohhhh! My damn head! What the…god… ok, let me have it." The Chief hadn't forgotten the all-business demeanor of the former head of the Other investigation. This wasn't likely to be a friendly postcard.

"No, don't let me have it. You open it, Professor. My head can't take any bad news today. If it's bad news, just don't even tell me. You didn't see me. You tried to give me the message, but I went home sick. That's it. I'll take a sick day! I'm out…"

He tried to rise, and then slumped back down into his well-worn, brown leather chair.

"What's in it?"

The Professor remembered the intimidating Brandon himself, and opened the envelope like he was disarming a bomb. The large man's hands actually shook as he read what was inside.

Then, he made a quizzical expression, and put his hand to his face, and then, despite his best effort to keep it inside, he let out the loudest laugh anyone had ever heard come out of the Professor's mouth.

"Hee Hee Hee HEEEE!" the large man's squeaky bray of a laugh could be heard through multiple layers of office walls.

"Give me that goddamn envelope," and then Chief looked inside…his eyes widened like an owl's…and then he just put his head down and chuckled like he was being tickled from head to toe.

"Goddamn," he kept saying. "Goddamn."

Inside the envelope was an official black folder. A folder they'd seen before — seen before when they first met Agent Brandon. A folder marked "Letters of Authorization". Brandon had pulled out this folder when she first took charge of the investigation team. Brandishing this folder, she threatened to have every one of those in attendance fired, drafted, or arrested if they so much as looked at her the wrong way. She told everyone the letters inside that folder gave her that ultimate authority. And, after that, not a single person on the team dared cross her. Wouldn't even think of it.

"LETTERS OF AUTHORIZATION" it said in big, bold, official print right across the front. Only, now the folder had a Post-It on it. The Post-It said "the truth is out there."

Inside the folder were 12 sheets of paper…

…they were all blank.

END

Bernie Nofel has been an inspiring contributor to San Diego's writing community for years. As a member of Writers Ink, Write Real Early, and Thursday Writers, Bernie has enthralled peers and audiences with his unique story-telling ability. When he isn't spinning tautly-woven, spellbinding, suspenseful yarns, he finds joy as a professional theater actor, grant writer, college instructor, and communication consultant.

Bernie has a gift for unwrapping stories that are given to him like birthday presents - he unfolds what's gradually revealed to him, layer by layer, and is just as surprised as anyone else with what's inside.

Sometimes, what's inside turns out to be something very ... different....

He promises you'll want to re-read this thriller, all over again!